Eliz...

righ...

Very ... to the elevator and rode up beside the diminutive Officer Ruiz. Elizabeth was a person of interest to him despite the fact that he had broken his own rules and crossed the line with her, a line he had sworn to himself that he would never cross.

And he hadn't.

Not until that night in Nevada when they had wound up stranded thanks to an untimely thunderstorm.

He'd been drawn to Elizabeth from the first moment he'd seen her that day she came to work for his father. He couldn't take his eyes off her.

But he more than anyone knew that business and pleasure had to be kept at arm's length from one another. Otherwise, mixing the two together was just asking for trouble.

But none of that had been on his mind that night in Nevada. All he could think of was how very much he wanted her.

***

Be sure to check out the rest of the books in
The Adair Affairs miniseries—The Adair Affairs:
The notorious and powerful political family is back
with even more secrets.

***

If you're on Twitter, tell us what you
think of Harlequin Romantic Suspense!
#harlequinromsuspense

Dear Reader,

The morning of January 15, 1983, I was seven months pregnant with my second child. My husband had recently been laid off from his aerospace job and my mother had died suddenly after what was supposed to be a simple surgery. I was having a very difficult time tapping into optimism. But then my husband came into the bathroom to tell me that my agent, Pat Teal, was on the phone. I assumed she was calling with yet another rejection. I wasn't sure I was up to taking the call. But my mother had taught me to always take life head-on, so I took the call.

Pat told me, "She said it was perfect." The "she" was Karen Solem, the head of Silhouette Books (later to join Harlequin). The "it" was my proposal for a Silhouette Desire entitled *Tried and True*. And "perfect" was what my life was about to become (okay, *near* perfect) with this very precious first sale.

That was 249 books ago. What you have in front of you is number 250, and I'm just as excited about writing it as I was writing that first one. Sometimes I think that this is all a dream and that I'm going to wake up soon to find myself lying in a pool of ever-growing rejection slips. But so far, so good.

As ever, I thank you for reading this book, and from the bottom of my heart, I wish you someone to love who loves you back.

All the best,

Marie Ferrarella

CARRYING
HIS SECRET

Marie Ferrarella

HARLEQUIN® ROMANTIC SUSPENSE

Special thanks and acknowledgment to Marie Ferrarella
for her contribution to The Adair Affairs miniseries.

ISBN-13: 978-0-373-27905-0

Carrying His Secret

Copyright © 2015 by Harlequin Books S.A.

Recycling programs
for this product may
not exist in your area.

Printed in U.S.A.

About the Author

This *USA TODAY* bestselling and RITA® Award–winning author has written 250 books for Harlequin, some under the name Marie Nicole. Her romances are beloved by fans worldwide. Visit her website, marieferrarella.com.

Books by Marie Ferrarella

HARLEQUIN ROMANTIC SUSPENSE

Cavanaugh Justice

The Cavanaugh Code
In Bed with the Badge
Cavanaugh Judgment
Cavanaugh Reunion
A Cavanaugh Christmas
Cavanaugh's Bodyguard
Cavanaugh Rules
Cavanaugh's Surrender
Cavanaugh on Duty
Mission: Cavanaugh Baby
Cavanaugh Hero
Cavanaugh Undercover
Cavanaugh Strong

Visit the Author Profile page at
Harlequin.com for more titles

With undying gratitude to everyone who ever read one of my books, then went back to read another—thank you.
You made all this possible.

&

With love to Patience Bloom
for always being in my corner.

Prologue

A woman's piercing scream shattered the evening silence.

Filling up all the spaces within the very modern glass-enclosed executive office, the sound seemed to grow in volume rather than abate as seconds went by.

Cringing in response, Reginald Adair's executive assistant, Elizabeth Shelton, didn't immediately realize that the terrified scream had come from her. Shock, horror and disbelief had wrapped themselves so tightly around her consciousness that she wasn't aware of anything except for the body lying in a pool of blood on the two-hundred-dollar-a-square-foot carpet.

Reginald Adair's body.

Handsome, dynamic Reginald Adair, president of AdAir Corp, a huge cellular company that provided signal bars for close to two-thirds of the country thanks to its numerous satellites circling the earth, lay crumpled and unresponsive on the floor of his glass-and-chrome executive office.

This wasn't happening. This couldn't be happening.

Pull yourself together, Lizzy. The man needs help, not drama, Elizabeth admonished herself. It didn't matter that she felt like throwing up. This wasn't about her. This was about saving Adair.

It felt as if every square inch of her five-foot-seven body was trembling as she knelt down beside the man. At sixty-two and an inch shy of being six feet tall, Adair had prided himself on keeping in excellent shape.

He might have been in excellent shape, but he was also heavy. Definitely not an easy man to move.

Bracing herself, through sheer determination, Elizabeth somehow managed to turn the man over onto his back.

His eyes were closed and there was blood flowing from a hole in his chest.

It took everything Elizabeth had for her not to back away. Another scream bubbled up in her throat. She pressed her lips together to keep it from emerging.

Taking a deep breath to brace herself, she searched for any sign of life. A panicky feeling was only inches away from erupting.

"Mr. Adair, can you hear me?"

For exactly sixty seconds, it felt as if every single thought had fled her head, leaving the entire area of her brain completely empty.

And then, because she'd been independent and on her own for most of her life, Elizabeth snapped out of the encroaching malaise.

Searching for his heartbeat, the only thing Elizabeth felt was her own as it went into overdrive, thundering madly against her rib cage.

"Think, damn it. Think!" Elizabeth frantically ordered out loud, desperate to keep it together. But what could she possibly do to save him?

Splaying her hand across her boss's bloodied chest, she thought she detected just the faintest whisper of a heartbeat. At first she was afraid to push against it, afraid to make it beat any harder than it was because she was concerned that the pressure would make Adair lose more blood that much faster.

Tugging her cardigan off, she wadded up the sweater and then pressed it against the hole in Adair's chest, frantically trying to stop the flow of blood.

Her own heart almost stopped when she saw his eyelids flutter.

"Oh, thank God. You *are* alive," Elizabeth cried. "Stay with me, Mr. Adair, stay with me," she begged.

She saw the light of recognition enter his vividly blue eyes. His lips began to move, but he made no audible sound.

Bending over him, Elizabeth brought her ear closer to Adair's lips, trying to make out the words he was saying. He was so weak she could hardly feel his breath on her face as he attempted to tell her something.

Was it the name of his attacker? Had he seen who had done this to him?

Straining, Elizabeth still couldn't make any of the words out.

"What? I'm sorry, sir, I can't hear you," Elizabeth told him.

He struggled again to say something, but still nothing came out.

She needed help.

Adrenaline racing through every fiber of her being, Elizabeth continued pressing on Adair's wound with one hand as she searched for her cell phone in her purse with the other.

Her phone was in her shoulder bag. It *had* to be, Elizabeth thought as the phone continued to avoid her questing fingers.

Finally, in frustration, she took the strap in her

teeth to facilitate keeping the purse open while she used her free hand to upend it.

Wallet, keys, her AdAir ID badge, along with her cell phone, came raining down beside her. Grabbing the phone, Elizabeth quickly dialed 9-1-1.

Within a couple of seconds, a cheerful, competent-sounding female voice declared, "Nine-one-one, what is your emergency?"

A torrent of rambling words threatened to pour out of her mouth all at once. Elizabeth struggled to sound coherent. "I need an ambulance. Now."

"Are you hurt, ma'am?" the voice asked calmly.

"No, no, it's not me. It's for my boss. Someone shot my boss."

The woman wouldn't know who her boss was. Elizabeth knew she had to elaborate, but she had trouble finding the words and slowing her breath enough to speak.

She tried again. "Reginald Adair's been shot. Executive suite, top floor of AdAir Corp." She all but gasped out the words. "Please hurry!"

Elizabeth dragged in a ragged breath, doing her level best not to sound like someone having a meltdown. Breaking down now wouldn't help save Mr. Adair.

"Do you know who shot him?" the woman on the other end asked.

The routine question, asked so calmly, filled Elizabeth with unreasonable anger.

"No, I don't know who," she snapped. "Don't you think that would be the first thing I told you if I knew who did it?" Her hostile words echoed in her brain. Elizabeth forced herself to calm down. "He's still breathing. Please. Send someone quickly."

Everyone knew where the sleek six-story chrome-and-glass building was located, but she rattled off the address anyway.

"Please, I don't know how much time he has left. There's blood everywhere." Elizabeth could almost swear she felt Adair slipping away from beneath her hand even as she spoke to the 9-1-1 operator. "You need to send an ambulance *now*."

"They're already on their way, ma'am," the woman told her. "Stay on the line with me until they come," she coaxed.

Elizabeth was about to tell the 9-1-1 operator that she'd stay on as long as she could when she saw Reginald's eyes begin to glaze over.

No, no, no, no! Please don't die, Elizabeth silently pleaded.

"His chest isn't moving," Elizabeth cried out loud, panic mounting in her voice again. "I can't feel his chest moving. He's not breathing!"

Dropping the phone, she began to do chest

compressions using both hands. "Open your eyes again, Mr. Adair. Please! Open your eyes for me."

But no matter how hard she pushed on his chest, she could barely detect that faint whisper of a heartbeat she'd initially felt.

Doubling up her fist, she began to pound on Adair's bloodied chest, remembering something she'd once witnessed being done in a documentary.

The distant sound of a siren penetrated the wall of panic and heavy breathing, both coming from her.

"They're coming, Mr. Adair. I can hear them. They're coming. Just hang on a little longer and they'll save you. Just a little longer, please," she begged.

The man on the rug, his body partially outlined in a growing pool of his own blood, remained very, very still. There was no longer any indication that he was alive.

Refusing to accept that the man she had worked for so faithfully for the past five years was beyond hearing her, Elizabeth continued to pound on his chest.

She was still pounding when the paramedics arrived at his office.

"Come on, come on, you can do this. You can

cheat death. You're larger-than-life, Mr. Adair. Work with me here! *Please!*"

But a few seconds later there was no rhythm of any sort beating beneath her hands.

Chapter 1

An hour ago, Elizabeth Shelton had been driving out of AdAir Corp's underground parking facility and on her way to her weekend.

It was eight o'clock on a Friday night and the rest of the employees who worked at AdAir Corp, one of the country's leading cell phone providers, had already left for their weekends. Today the mass exodus had taken place at five o'clock, because that was when the building's surveillance cameras had all been turned off. They'd had to leave, for safety reasons. A memo had gone out, and everyone knew that the existing system was being upgraded.

Elizabeth had stayed behind in order to catch up on some last-minute work. Work she needed to have prepared and at her fingertips for a meeting she was attending on Monday morning in her boss's place. Reginald Adair was scheduled to be out of town on a business trip. He should have already left at six to catch his flight.

Preoccupied with something she had just learned earlier in the day—something that was going to completely upend her world once it became public knowledge…and it *was going* to become public knowledge, because that was the nature of the beast—Elizabeth had neglected to take several very important papers with her when she'd left the office. Without those papers her weekend would be completely unproductive despite the reams of papers she *did* have in her briefcase.

She'd gotten halfway down the block, reviewing everything she needed to have taken with her, when she realized her mistake. The papers that were the key to the entire presentation were still sitting on her side desk, waiting to be packed up in her briefcase.

Muttering a few choice words under her breath about the state of her mind, Elizabeth had executed a narrow U-turn and driven straight back to the underground parking facility.

Habit had her easing her vehicle into her designated parking space—not that she needed to stick to protocol tonight. There were no other cars on her level—or on any other level, she strongly suspected—because everyone else had gone home, or at least away from here, three hours ago.

She had to get herself under control, Elizabeth had silently lectured as she walked across the parking structure to the private executive elevator that only let out on the sixth floor. Her situation was what it was, and she was not about to do anything drastic to change it. That just wasn't her way.

In the meantime, she couldn't allow her dilemma to upset her to the point that she wasn't able to do her job.

God knew she was going to need the money in the coming months. And besides, work was all she really had. She couldn't take a chance on losing her job.

She'd laughed at herself then, as she got on the private elevator. Months? Was she kidding herself? It was more like *years*. She was going to need money—extra money—for years to come. Eighteen at the very least.

Most likely longer than that.

Later. She'd think about it later, she'd told herself. For now she just needed to get those missing papers and go home.

One step at a time, Lizzy. One step at a time will get you there. Wherever there is.

The elevator had come to a stop, its stainless steel doors sliding apart soundlessly. Waiting for her to get off.

Stepping out, Elizabeth hurried toward her office, which was just beyond her boss's.

The light coming from beneath Reginald Adair's door registered in her peripheral vision and had caught her attention a beat after she passed it.

It made her stop in her tracks.

Reginald Adair was supposed to be on his way to the airport if not actually aboard the plane by now. Had he left without remembering to shut off the lights?

That wasn't like him, she thought. The man was nothing if not extremely precise. He believed in leading by example and that meant following all the rules, no matter how small the rule might seem. That included powering down his computer and turning off the lights when he left the office for the night.

Approaching the closed office door, Elizabeth had knocked lightly at first. Receiving no response, she'd knocked a little louder, and this time she'd called out to him so he could hear her through the door.

"Mr. Adair, it's Elizabeth. Do you need me to take care of anything for you before I leave the office for the weekend?"

She'd looked down at her watch. "Is everything

okay? Your flight is leaving soon. Would you like me to call a cab for you?"

She'd leaned her ear against the door to see if she could hear anything and that was when she felt the door move slightly beneath her cheek.

The door had been left unlocked and open.

If he was there, why wasn't he answering her? And if he wasn't there, why had he left all the lights on as well as the door unlocked? Perhaps in his rush to get to the airport, he had forgotten? But the man had never been late for anything in the entire five years she had worked for him.

A wave of uneasiness slipped over her.

Something wasn't making sense.

Bracing herself, Elizabeth had gingerly pushed opened the door with her fingertips. That it gave so easily should have warned her that something was drastically wrong.

But with her own personal dilemma fresh and foremost on her mind, she had completely missed that sign. That in turn had left her completely unprepared to find Reginald Adair sprawled out on the floor of his office the way that she had.

Elizabeth had been even *less* prepared to be catapulted from her role as the executive assistant to the president of AdAir Corp, to a person of interest in the very same corporate president's lethal attack.

An aura of disbelief encircled her. It felt as if

the whole world around her had transformed into a surreal setting that made absolutely no sense to her, no matter how hard she tried to put the puzzle pieces together.

The first detective on the scene, a fifteen-year veteran named Otis Kramer, lost no time in firing questions at her.

At first she'd just assumed that the questions were routine, but as they kept coming, Elizabeth began to change her mind.

Her uneasiness intensified.

When the detective, who was married to his job, continued interrogating her, Elizabeth couldn't keep the nausea tamped down any longer.

"I need to use the ladies' room," she'd told the slope-shouldered man in the ill-fitting, off-the-rack charcoal-gray suit. "I think I'm going to be sick."

There wasn't an ounce of compassion in the man's thin, nondescript face. "When we're done," he'd snapped back.

"Unless you're okay with having your shoes ruined, *now*," she'd countered.

She was certain that if she wasn't allowed access to the bathroom immediately, she was going to throw up right there, at the crime scene. Thankfully, the man's eyes widened and he nodded his head slightly. With that, Elizabeth quickly turned on her heel and rushed to Reginald Adair's private bathroom. The disgruntled-looking detective was right behind her.

Entering the spacious restroom, she began to close the door behind her, only to have the detective put his hand in the way, effectively stopping the door from shutting him out.

Her patience just about worn down to a nub, Elizabeth glared at the rumpled older man. "In case you failed to notice, we are on the sixth floor. I'm not about to crawl out the window."

He glared back at her for another moment or two, then reluctantly released the door.

Just in time as far as Elizabeth was concerned. Rushing over to the toilet, she sank down on her knees in front of the bowl.

The contents of her stomach from the past few hours made a reappearance in recycled form.

After everything she could have possibly eaten spilled out—and then some—Elizabeth pulled herself up to her feet again. Standing before the marble sink, she gave herself a minute to recover, then turned on the faucet and threw cold water on her face. The face looking back at her in the mirror was almost a ghastly shade of white.

White sheets were darker than she currently was.

Get it together, Lizzy, she told her reflection. *You look too guilty. That detective will be all over you like a starving dog on a bone.*

Elizabeth gave herself a couple of extra minutes to pull herself together before she opened the door. Kramer was standing right in front of it. She barely avoided walking right into him.

Determined to look as if she was in control, Elizabeth told the detective, "I'm sorry about that. I can answer the rest of your questions now."

Kramer was obviously annoyed that she had managed to put him off, no matter what the reason. He looked far from friendly.

The next minute, he was gesturing at her to stand over to the side as the gurney carrying Reginald Adair moved past them. Instead of paramedics, the gurney was accompanied by two men from the coroner's office.

Her heart felt like lead in her chest.

Adair hadn't made it, Elizabeth realized, startled. Somehow, maybe because the man always seemed larger-than-life to her, she'd expected him to recover no matter what the wound.

Tears sprang to her eyes, threatening to fall. She did what she could to hold them back. Tears weren't going to help the man now.

Nothing was.

Flat brown eyes took inventory of her, moving from top to bottom. "There's a lot of blood on you," the detective finally commented.

Completely oblivious to her appearance, Elizabeth looked down at herself for the first time since she'd found Adair on the floor.

The entire bottom portion of her skirt, as well as large sections of her blouse, was stained with blood. Reginald Adair's blood.

The realization—not to mention the sight of that blood—brought a chill racing up and down her spine.

"I guess it got all over me when I was trying to revive him," she told the detective numbly.

"You tried to revive him," the detective echoed. "Even though he was dead?"

The latter part of the question was all but fired at her. The detective continued staring at her, his eyes nearly boring small holes into her.

"He wasn't dead at the time," Elizabeth snapped irritably. Too much had happened in too short of a time frame. She wasn't up to coping with a rude police detective who seemed to have made up his mind that she was guilty of murdering her boss and had condemned her right from the start. "I detected a faint heartbeat and tried to get his heart to beat harder, stronger." She blew out a breath as she wrapped her arms around herself, feeling suddenly cold, wishing there was someone else in the room, someone familiar she could turn to for moral support as she suffered through this entire ordeal, even just for a moment or two. "I didn't succeed," she ended quietly.

Kramer snorted and looked at her pointedly. "Now there's an understatement." The comment was accompanied by a dry, humorless laugh. "What were you doing in the building in the first place?" he wanted to know. "I couldn't help but notice that the entire building was empty except for you two."

"Mr. Adair gave the order for everyone to leave by five," she told him. Maybe this would go faster if she just answered him in simple sentences, she thought, desperate to have this over with. She had calls to make, people to notify of this terrible tragedy.

"Convenient." Kramer continued to stare at her intently, waiting for her to break or say something out of turn.

"Not really." She knew her tone sounded defensive, but there was something about the detective that just brought out the worst in her. "Mr. Adair was having the security system overhauled and updated."

The detective's face was expressionless. "How many people knew about that?"

Wasn't he listening? "Everyone," she answered, trying not to allow her exasperation to poke through. "That's why they all left at five."

"Not all." Kramer looked at her pointedly. "You stayed."

"I had something to finish. It took longer than I

thought," Elizabeth told him, leaving out the part explaining *why* it took longer: because she was so preoccupied with this new situation she unwillingly found herself in. "When I finished, I left the building," she informed him coolly, then added, "It was around eight o'clock."

"You left," he echoed. "And yet, you're here. Why is that?" Kramer asked, keeping his voice deceptively light, almost friendly sounding.

Elizabeth didn't know if the detective was mocking her or trying to trip her up into making some kind of a confession. In either case, she trod very carefully, knowing that any misstep would have the man pouncing on her with who knew what sort of accusations—not the least of which would be naming her to be Reginald Adair's killer.

She phrased her explanation about her reappearance as simply as possible. "I realized that I'd left a few pages I was going to need on my desk, so I came back for them."

Kramer stared at her as if he was x-raying her very bones. "So you were planning on working this weekend."

His tone was too pleasant. She didn't trust it. "Yes, I was."

Kramer circled her slowly, as if taking measure of her from all sides. "An attractive woman like you, staying home all weekend, working—what's wrong with this picture?" he asked, standing in front of her again.

It was obvious that he didn't believe her, Elizabeth thought. She was telling him the truth and the detective didn't believe her.

Was she going to need a lawyer on top of everything else that had happened today?

She knew that if she showed the least bit of fear in the face of this interrogation, she'd be lost.

Raising her chin, she tossed her long blond hair over her shoulder and said defiantly, "Nothing, if that woman wants to get ahead in the company. It takes a great deal of hard work."

Kramer shrugged, his loose-fitting jacket shifting on his thin shoulders. "Another way might be sleeping with the boss," he suggested.

That might be the way you'd do it, but I wouldn't, Elizabeth thought angrily.

For now, the response had to remain solely in her head, since saying anything remotely antagonistic out loud would be asking for trouble and far from wise.

"Mr. Adair is—*was*," Elizabeth corrected herself, "a married man with a family," she pointed out to the detective, hoping that would be the end of his condescending inference.

Even so, she couldn't deny that she felt guilty—and perhaps even partially responsible—for Adair's death. Maybe if she'd just stopped by earlier…

Turning, she watched the gurney being guided by the coroner's men until it disappeared into the private elevator car.

"I should have checked on him," she murmured to herself.

Kramer's ears went up on high alert. "What did you say?" he asked, his eyes once more boring into her.

She wanted to shout at the man to leave her alone. Instead, she patiently explained her meaning.

"Before I left the first time, I should have checked on Mr. Adair then. He was supposed to have already left for a business trip—that's why I came into his office in the first place. I saw the light coming from underneath his door. It should have been off and he should have been at the airport, waiting to take off," she added mournfully.

And now he never will.

"Looks like he found another way to take off," Kramer commented, his tone far from friendly or compassionate.

Elizabeth pitied anyone who had to work with this man. "Am I free to go?" she wanted to know. The detective made her very uneasy, not to mention the fact that she desperately wanted to get out of her bloodied clothes and into an accommodating hot shower.

"Sure," he said magnanimously. But when she

turned to leave, he qualified, "When we're done." His tone made her blood run cold. "I've still got a few more questions for you."

The smile that slid over his thin lips was completely disembodied from anything remotely personal, warm or sincere.

"Why don't you come down to the station with me where you can be more comfortable?" he suggested.

"Come into my parlor," said the spider to the fly, Elizabeth thought with a sense of uneasiness. The old familiar phrase immediately ran through her head.

Who in their right mind thought that a police station was a comfortable place to spend their evening?

"If you don't mind, why don't we just go into my office?" Elizabeth suggested instead. "It's right next to Mr. Adair's."

To show the detective how close it was, she pointed to it and then mentally crossed her fingers that he would agree to it.

The last place she wanted to go was a police station. She was tired, upset and she had a number of people to notify. Going to the police station would just needlessly use up more time.

"I do mind," Kramer replied. His barely open eyes—like the slits of a reptile's—looked at her for a long moment before the detective told her, "I do better on my own home turf. You understand," he added loftily.

No, she didn't, Elizabeth thought as she allowed herself to be escorted out of Reginald Adair's office. She didn't understand anything that had transpired today. Not who would have killed Mr. Adair, or why, not to mention how they could have done it without her hearing *anything*. She was, after all, in the next office. Could they have done it in the short amount of time she was gone from the building?

Most of all, she couldn't understand why the police detective thought of her as a possible suspect—and he most certainly did think of her that way, judging by the look in his eyes when he was staring at her.

Aside from proximity, which might cover opportunity, the most important factor in a homicide was conspicuously missing in this particular instance.

Namely, she had absolutely no motive to kill her boss.

Adair had never been anything but kind and fair to her in the years that she had worked for him. While she knew that Reginald Adair had his flaws—who didn't?—whenever he interacted with her, the man had never been anything but upstanding and kind.

She'd found herself admiring Adair's work ethic

and felt that AdAir Corporation was a very good place for her to work. There was an energy here, a zest that promised good things came of efforts that were put forth.

Nowhere within all that was there anything that even distantly resembled a motive.

Rather than just allow herself to be blindly herded out of the building, Elizabeth turned to the detective as they got into the elevator and demanded point-blank, "Am I a suspect?"

She tried not to dwell on the fact that they were riding down in the same private elevator that had just taken away Adair's lifeless body.

"You catch on fast," Kramer commented, slanting only a side glance at her.

"Why?" She wanted to know. "Why am I a suspect—other than the fact that I was the one who found the body," she added.

Kramer nodded and what looked like a smug expression filtered over his face.

"That'll do it," he told her, then paused dramatically. "Do you know how many killers actually call in to report their crimes? They like inserting themselves into the crime scene. What better way to do it than to find the body and call it in? It gives them an excuse to hang around."

"No, I have no idea how many," Elizabeth replied, her calm voice at odds with the huge knot in her stomach. "All I know is that I'm not one of them."

"We'll see," Kramer replied. Whistling, he got off the elevator, then turned and waited for her to catch up. "After you," he said grandly, taking hold of her arm and hustling her toward his car.

This is a nightmare, Elizabeth couldn't help thinking. And it was only getting steadily worse.

Chapter 2

An entire storm of emotions was spinning around within him at speeds that rivaled those attained by twisters and hurricanes.

If someone had asked him to describe exactly what it was that he was feeling, Whit Adair would have been forced to say, "Numb."

He was numb.

Numb and perhaps, for the first time in his life, more than a little lost. As the vice president of AdAir Corp, as well as the oldest of Reginald Adair's children, Whit was accustomed to being in charge and able to handle every situation he encountered.

It wasn't something that he'd schooled himself

to do, it was just something that had evolved naturally over time—because he knew that his father expected it of him and he both idolized and adored his father. He wanted to please the man. It had never occurred to him to behave in any other fashion.

Over the years, Whit had strongly nurtured the hope that someday his father would see him as a trusted asset and actually *say* as much. More than anything else, he'd longed to hear his father acknowledging the fact that he wasn't just good at what he did, he was damn near excellent. He would have sold his soul in exchange for a little praise from his father.

But now that was never going to happen.

He'd been on his way to the ranch, where he spent most weekends, when the phone call came. Some detective, whose name he heard but that failed to register, said that the police were trying to locate him.

"Is something wrong, detective?" he'd asked, a strange premonition slipping over him.

"I'm afraid so, sir. Where are you? I'd like to meet in person."

His place in San Diego was closer and he regarded it as less of a sanctuary, so he gave the detective his address. They arrived at the building almost simultaneously.

The detective looked as if he was worn out. Perhaps as a result of years of having to give unwelcome news to victim's families, Whit thought. "I'm afraid your father's been shot. He didn't make it."

Whit stared at the detective. He remembered noticing that the man had a small stain on his tie and thinking that the man's wife—if he had one—was going to berate him for being sloppy.

Strange the thoughts that went through your head when your whole world was shaken up, Whit thought. The detective had said something about taking him to view "the body"—as if that was now his father's new station in life; the body rather than Reginald Adair—offer to drive him. But he wanted some sort of control over the situation, so he had said he was going to drive himself. Giving him his card, the detective told him he'd lead the way, which was good because he had no idea where the morgue was.

His mind kept jumping around, going back and forth between the present and less than an hour ago.

Grief pressed against his chest like a giant lead weight.

He was never going to get the chance to bond with his father the way he'd always secretly hoped and, yes, *dreamed* that he would.

Someone had stolen that opportunity from him. Someone had murdered his father.

Someone was going to pay.

Whit swerved, narrowly avoiding a head-on collision with an SUV that jumped the light.

Damn it, Whit, get ahold of yourself!

For the life of him, Whit couldn't remember getting into his car. Moreover, he couldn't really remember the name of the detective whose card was in his pocket.

The man he was now following to the morgue.

The man who had said those awful words to him: *There's been a murder.*

And just like that, his entire life was put on hold as chaos took immediate possession of his brain. Everything else in his life—the myriad of details, the pending launch of new cellular software—all of it had taken a backseat to this horrendous event.

And now he was going to the morgue to identify the man who had been found shot dead in his father's ultramodern office.

He wasn't sure if he was going to be able to get through it.

There was glass separating him from the lifeless form on the gurney. Glass and a white sheet.

Bracing himself, Whit nodded and the attendant—probably the medical examiner's assistant, he assumed—gently pulled back the sheet from the deceased's face.

He hadn't braced himself enough.

Seeing his father like that, lifeless and so in-

credibly pale, was a horrible shock to his entire
system.

"Yes, that's him. That's my father."

His voice sounded almost disembodied to his
own ear. The words echoed in his head, torment-
ing him, long after they had faded from the air.

"Would you like to take a moment?" the detective asked.

No, he wouldn't like to take a moment. A moment wouldn't help. A thousand moments wouldn't
help, Whit thought angrily. There was only one
thing that would.

Turning away from the glass partition, he
looked at the detective and asked, "Do you know
who did this to him?"

"The investigation's just started," the detective
replied.

"So you've got nothing," Whit concluded.

"We do have a person of interest at the precinct who's being questioned right now," the man
offered.

Whit's blue eyes, normally so brilliant, were
almost flat as he asked, "Who is it?"

"Sir, we can't discuss an ongoing investigation,"
the detective said, nervously hiding behind regu-
lations.

Whit had been trained to detect weakness and
uncertainty in any and all opponents. That had
been his father's doing. Whit could tell now that

the detective was a man who could be bullied into complying—to an extent.

"You can if that investigation involved my father. Now who is being questioned?" he asked the man more forcefully.

The detective shrugged, as if conducting an internal debate with himself. "I guess you'll find out soon enough. It's your father's assistant. Elizabeth Shelton."

Whit stared at the man as if he had lost his mind. "Elizabeth Shelton?" he repeated incredulously. The one he'd taken numerous business trips with—the one who stirred his soul, although that was something he never intended to admit.

What the detective was suggesting just wasn't possible.

The detective nodded, anticipating the next question: *Why?* "She was the one who found the body and called it in."

A barrage of words rose to Whit's tongue like a band of angry villagers storming the manor carrying pitchforks and torches, but he didn't intend to waste his breath or his time on the detective. He needed to be elsewhere.

"Where is she being questioned?" he asked.

"At the police station. Detective Kramer is handling the case. Otis Kramer," the other man all but shouted after Whit as the latter hurried to the elevator.

* * *

This was insane, Whit thought over and over again as he hurried to the police station. Completely insane. Elizabeth could no more have killed his father than he could. Whit gripped his steering wheel, channeling his anger, doing his best to regain control over himself. He had to put an end to this farce and get Elizabeth out of there.

He owed it to both her and his father to put an end to the interrogation that was being conducted.

That he had to come to what amounted to her rescue was, in itself, only adding to his internal turmoil.

He'd been avoiding his father's executive assistant these last few weeks. Totally avoiding any one-on-one contact with her, avoiding even being in the same room as the woman. He had wanted to work a few things through first.

But his feelings in regard to being possibly confronted and maybe even redressed by Elizabeth were trumped by this unimaginably bizarre situation. Just because he hadn't summoned the courage to face her didn't excuse him from coming to her aid and extracting her from being interrogated by some overeager detective looking to make lieutenant.

Doing the speed limit and above, Whit arrived at the police station in what amounted to record time. A part of him had been expecting to be pulled over at any moment and given a speeding ticket. Luckily for him, San Diego's finest were otherwise occupied tonight.

Parking his silver-gray sports car in the lot's first row, Whit got out of the vehicle and dashed up the concrete front steps, then hurried into the building.

The interior of the precinct was alive with multiple activities, all going on at once. Even so, it was obvious that the murder of Reginald Adair was taking precedence over everything else.

Whit was grateful—if such a feeling could be put into play at a time like this—that the media hadn't come crawling out of the woodwork yet. One less obstacle for him to deal with.

But they would. They would most definitely come out of the woodwork. He knew that it was just a matter of time before this whole thing became a giant media circus, three rings and all.

The desk sergeant looked up just as Whit approached him. The grumpy expression on the heavyset man's face melted away as recognition set in. AdAir Corp—its president in particular— made large annual contributions to the policemen's fund. That earned the company—and especially Whit—respect as well as pledges of complete cooperation should the need arise.

It had arisen.

"We were all very sorry to hear about your father, Mr. Adair," O'Hara, the desk sergeant, told him, rising in his chair to shake his hand.

"Thank you," Whit answered, doing his best not to snap the response out. He wanted to move on to the reason why he was here at the precinct, not discuss his father's murder. "You're holding my father's assistant, Elizabeth Shelton, for questioning," he began.

"Yeah, that's right." The sergeant looked up from the ledger he was checking. "Ruiz," he called out, stopping the first uniformed policeman who walked by at that moment. "Take Mr. Adair upstairs to where Kramer's questioning that person of interest."

Elizabeth was a person of interest all right, Whit thought, falling into step beside the officer. A person of interest to *him*.

Very much so, he thought ruefully as he got into the elevator and rode up beside the diminutive Officer Ruiz. Elizabeth was a person of interest to him despite the fact that he had broken his own rules and crossed the line with her, a line he had sworn to himself that he would never cross.

And he hadn't.

Not for five years.

Not until that night in Nevada when they'd wound up stranded thanks to an untimely thunderstorm.

Stranded, attracted to one another, with just a

little too much to drink—it was a recipe for disaster. He realized that he'd been doomed right from the very start.

It had turned out to be a very volatile combination—for both of them.

Neither one of them, in his estimation, had imbibed enough to be considered drunk—but they had consumed just enough to have the carefully constructed walls around their professional relationship turn into tissue paper.

For his part, he'd been drawn to Elizabeth from the first moment he'd seen her that day she came to work for his father. He hadn't been able to take his eyes off her.

But he more than anyone knew that business and pleasure had to be kept at arm's length from one another. Mixing the two together was just asking for trouble—with a capital *T*.

But none of that had been on his mind that night in Nevada. All he'd been able to think of was how very much he wanted her.

Outside their hotel window, the wind had howled and the rain had lashed angrily against the glass panes. Inside, though, they had managed to create their own private haven. For the space of one magical night, he'd found himself coming as close to experiencing total perfection as he could ever hope.

Even so, morning had come with its heavy mantle of guilt. He had let his guard down. Moreover, he had taken advantage of the situation and of her. There was no excuse for that.

At a loss for how to handle it, he'd felt that his only recourse was to behave as if nothing had happened.

Elizabeth had done the same, which was why he was certain that refusing to acknowledge that anything had changed between them was the right way to go.

The right way…even though he ached for her with every breath he took.

But that was his problem, not hers, and Whit was resigned to spending the rest of his life dealing with that.

What he wasn't ready to do was spend the rest of his life without the man he'd looked up to and done his very best to emulate. Sure, for the most part, sons outlived their fathers, he knew that. But he wasn't ready for that to happen just yet.

Not like this.

Guess what? It happened. Deal with it, a voice inside his head ordered.

The stainless steel doors parted and he followed Officer Ruiz off the elevator and down the winding corridor.

The floor could have been deserted for all the attention Whit paid to what was going on all around him. He was focused on finding Elizabeth.

"Wait right here, Mr. Adair," the officer told him. "I'll let Detective Kramer know that you're here about the suspect."

Whit was *not* in the mood to hang back, waiting while the officer and the detective sorted things out. The turmoil within him was building up at an alarming rate, threatening to erupt at any moment unless he found some sort of an outlet. He didn't want to wind up yelling at anyone, but containing these emotions was becoming an increasingly difficult balancing act.

"I'll tell him myself," Whit informed the officer, moving ahead of Ruiz and letting himself into the room that the officer was about to open up.

His back to the door, Kramer snapped, "Not yet," thinking that he was being interrupted by one of the uniformed patrolmen.

"Yes, yet," Whit retorted coldly as he came in. At an imposing six feet two inches, Whit took command of any room he entered. The interrogation room was no exception.

Both the detective and the young woman he had been relentlessly questioning for the past hour turned in Whit's direction.

If there was a single point during the entire evening's events that she could have broken down and cried, Elizabeth thought, it would have been this very moment.

The man she had been determined to avoid until

she came to grips with her private situation had suddenly been cast in the role of a white knight.

Her white knight.

Elizabeth felt more conflicted than ever.

"Mr. Adair," she cried, remembering where they were and that their relationship was supposed to be strictly business and nothing more. To her credit, she was positive that no one else even suspected that they were anything more than two people who happened to work together and, on occasion, share a car.

He deliberately kept his face expressionless. "Elizabeth, are you all right?" he asked stiffly. With what amounted to great effort, Whit successfully suppressed the desire to sweep her into his arms and seek solace in hers.

She didn't answer his question. Instead, because she wasn't sure what he'd been told, she said, "Your father's gone. I am so sorry."

He wasn't about to respond to that or even react to it. He couldn't, not without breaking apart, and an Adair had to always remember to save face at all costs. So instead, he turned to the detective, his anger barely under control.

"What is Ms. Shelton doing here?" he demanded.

Obviously stunned at being challenged, Kramer was caught off guard.

"We had some questions," he began.

"So you decided to ask them in your interrogation room?" Whit wanted to know, his tone clearly indicating that the course Kramer had taken was completely unacceptable.

"I didn't want her distracted," Kramer answered coolly. After fifteen years, the detective felt he knew how to play the game.

It was a weak excuse at best and a lie at worst. Whit's brilliant blue eyes narrowed as he pinned the detective in place.

"Is Ms. Shelton being placed under arrest?" he wanted to know.

"No, but—" Kramer's voice cracked slightly at the obvious confrontation. He hadn't expected it to come from the family.

"Then if she's not under arrest, she's coming with me," Whit informed the detective. "Anyone with eyes can see that the woman's in shock, not to mention that she's in desperate need of a change of clothes."

"They offered me some sweat clothes," Elizabeth interjected, desperately struggling to keep from breaking down. "I think one of the officers just went to get them."

The information had no effect on Whit. "They shouldn't have brought you here in the first place," he said tersely, his eyes never leaving the detective's face.

Kramer had no use for people of privilege who

believed themselves to be above the law and allowed to do as they pleased.

"I'm not finished questioning her," Kramer informed Whit.

Whit was not about to back off. He wanted to get Elizabeth out of here. He had questions of his own he wanted to ask her, but first she needed to get away from the interrogation room.

"You are for now," Whit told him. Getting behind Elizabeth's chair, he took hold of the back and moved it out for her as she stood. "We're leaving, Detective," he told the other man. There was no room for argument with his tone. "If you have any further questions, Ms. Shelton will be happy to answer them after she's had a good night's sleep and a change of clothes." He barely spared her a glance as he said, "Let's go, Elizabeth."

Her legs felt wobbly as she walked out with Whit, but she suppressed the desire to take hold of his arm for support. Elizabeth was exceedingly relieved to get away from the detective, whose questions had come at an ever increasing rate as his tone grew more accusing.

But her sense of relief was in conflict with the sorrow she felt for the man standing beside her in the elevator.

Though she was certain that he didn't know it, she was aware of the case of hero worship that Whit harbored when it came to his father. Knew, too, that at least on the surface, her late boss had not demonstrated any sort of displays of affection for his son. For any of his children, really, except, from what she'd heard, his daughter. The youngest Adair appeared to be near and dear to the man.

"You should have called me," Whit told her the moment the doors closed, separating them from the rest of the police-crowded floor.

He sounded even more distant than usual, Elizabeth couldn't help thinking.

"The detective wouldn't let me," she told him. "He said I didn't need to make a phone call because I wasn't under arrest. According to him, we were only having a friendly discussion."

"Friendly?" Whit questioned.

"It's a new, really loose definition of the word," she said sarcastically. Elizabeth sighed deeply, relieved beyond words even though her heart was very heavy. "Thank you for coming to get me. How did you know I was here?"

"Some detectives came to notify me about Dad. They had me come to the morgue to make the official identification."

But she had already told them it was Reginald Adair, Elizabeth thought. "I guess my word wasn't good enough," she said with a shrug.

She would have wanted to spare Whit having to make the ID. Obviously the detective had had other ideas.

"You're not the next of kin, I am," Whit told her the next moment.

His voice was stony, as if he was doing his very best to keep any sliver of emotion as far away from him as possible, Elizabeth noted.

He hadn't been like that the night they'd found themselves all but trapped in the hotel room, held captive by a freak storm.

As if on cue, the warmth, the tenderness, the passion that she had experienced that night came rushing back to her. She'd had no idea that Whit was that sort of a lover. He was so different from the way he usually acted around her. If anything, she would have said he was repressed, keeping all his emotions under virtual lock and key, so well hidden that no one would ever suspect that the man had cupped her face with his hands and initially brushed his lips against hers as lightly as a falling petal floats to the ground when cradled by a spring breeze.

That had been the start of it all—and had led to so much more.

Her heart ached for him. She wished that there was something she could do to help.

But there was nothing.

Elizabeth stopped at the base of the stairs just before the relatively empty rear parking lot.

"Why are you stopping?" Whit wanted to know.

Her eyes met his. "Whit, I am so, so sorry," she whispered.

"Yeah, well, everyone dies sometime," he said with a careless shrug. Inside he was struggling to keep himself under control, but he had no intentions of exposing that part of himself to anyone. "The car's right over—"

He got no further than that, absently pointing in the general direction where he had parked his vehicle.

He got no further because at that moment, Elizabeth threw her arms around him, as much to comfort him as to *be* comforted by him. Her feelings of bereavement were enormous.

He'd been taught from a very young age not to show any emotion. That included responding to it if it came from anyone else.

Whit instinctively began to pull back.

Chapter 3

"I'm sorry," Whit said stiffly, successfully managing to suppress all signs of the internal tug-of-war that was going on within of him. "I'm not very good at comforting people."

Elizabeth forced a smile to her lips. "I'm not looking to be comforted," she told him. It was a lie, but right now, she felt something far larger was at stake here, namely the rest of the truth. "I'm trying to comfort *you*."

Her reply seemed to put him off even more than before. "Well, you don't have to bother. I'm all right," he proclaimed as he began heading toward his car again. "I'll take you home," he informed her just before he reached the vehicle.

The thought of going straight home was extremely appealing, but it would also leave her stranded the next morning. Intent on questioning her at the police station, Kramer had whisked her away in a squad car. Her own vehicle was sitting in the parking structure beneath the AdAir Corp building where she had left it.

"My car is still at AdAir Corp. If you don't mind, I need to be dropped off there," Elizabeth told him. Getting into the passenger seat of his sports car, she quickly secured her seat belt. "And you are *not* all right," she insisted as he put his key into the ignition. Just who did the man think he was kidding? "Your father was just murdered."

"I know," Whit replied, his voice distant and deadly calm. "I just had to identify his body." Before she could continue her outpouring of sympathy, sympathy he neither welcomed nor wanted, Whit steered the conversation in a different direction. "Why don't you tell me exactly what happened."

Elizabeth drew in a deep breath as they pulled away from the police station's rear parking lot. She slanted a look at his profile. "Are you asking me to tell you what I told the police?"

He considered the idea that she might have kept something back from the detective. After all, she was his father's executive assistant. Her loyalty lay with AdAir, and if something had happened tonight that might have put his father in a bad light, Whit felt rather confident that Elizabeth would either cover it up or omit it in her narrative in an attempt to preserve his father's good name.

"I want you to tell me what happened," Whit repeated evenly.

"That's not the same thing," Elizabeth pointed out. "I don't really *know* what happened," she told him truthfully. "I only know what I saw after the fact."

Maybe she was telling the truth, Whit thought. For now, he had no choice but to believe her.

"Then tell me that," he said.

His voice was so devoid of any emotion Elizabeth was certain that he was going to have a meltdown at any moment.

She continued looking at him, trying to penetrate the walls he had put up around himself. "It's not healthy to repress what you're feeling."

"I'm well aware of that." His tone was frosty as he cut her off, closing the topic. "You were going to tell me what you saw."

She couldn't reach him, Elizabeth thought. She felt helpless even as she understood that he was doing the only thing he felt he could do—employ a survival mechanism. It was obviously too early for him to deal with the feelings of loss his father's murder had unearthed within him.

She'd try to reach him later, Elizabeth promised herself. But now just wasn't the time.

Elizabeth focused on the events that had transpired earlier that evening.

"I had just pulled out of the parking area when I realized that I didn't have everything I needed to work on my presentation."

He spared her a quick look as he made a right turn. "Presentation?"

She nodded. "It's scheduled for Monday morning. I'm making it in your father's place," she explained. "He was going to be away on a business trip." Again she thought of the fact that she needed to call people, to cancel meetings and appointments.

Tomorrow, she'd do it all tomorrow. Tonight was for regrouping. And healing.

Whit frowned. He wasn't aware of any business trip, but his father didn't usually clear things with him, even if he was the corporation's vice president. His father had always had his own way of doing things. Like as not, those who worked in close proximity with Reginald Adair usually found things out after the fact. Whit supposed this presentation was to have been no different.

"Go on," he urged stoically.

She went over the events step-by-step, thinking that without the police breathing down her neck, maybe now she would remember something that had escaped her when she was being interrogated if she reviewed all her own movements.

"I made a U-turn and drove back into the parking structure. Almost everyone else had left at five o'clock, so the lot was practically empty. The security cameras were all down and your father felt that his people shouldn't have to be working in an unsecured building."

"I read the memo," Whit snapped curtly.

She looked at him for a long moment. "Sorry. I forgot."

Realizing that he was exceeding the speed limit, Whit eased his foot on the accelerator. He also reined in his temper.

"No, I'm sorry. I shouldn't have bitten your head off. Go on," he encouraged.

She picked up the narrative where she had dropped it. As she spoke, she could see the events transpiring before her all over again.

"I took the private executive elevator up to the sixth floor. Your father's door was closed, but the lights were still on. I knocked on his door to see if I could help him with whatever was still keeping him here. I knew he should have already left for the airport.

"When he didn't answer, I knocked again, then tried the doorknob. It wasn't locked." For a second, her breath caught in her throat as she relived the moment. "I pushed it open slowly." Elizabeth stopped for a moment, bracing herself against the words she was to utter next. "Your father was lying facedown on the rug. I think I screamed—I'm not sure," she confessed.

"Was he still—?" Whit couldn't bring himself to say the word.

She spared him that by quickly replying, "Alive? Yes, he was. I tried to stop the bleeding with my sweater, pressing it against the bullet wound, then I called nine-one-one. I performed CPR on your father until the paramedics came. But I couldn't save him," she said mournfully, taking full responsibility for his father's demise with those very words.

"It wasn't your fault," Whit told her stiffly, his body rigid as he stared straight ahead at the road.

"But it was," she argued. Whit glanced in her direction, clearly puzzled. "If I had come back earlier, maybe the killer wouldn't have killed your father."

"And maybe he would have killed you for being a witness to what he did," Whit countered, stating the fact as if he were reading chapter and verse out of a criminology textbook.

Despite his words, Elizabeth wasn't finished beating herself up. "I should have gone to your father before I left and asked him if he needed me to do something, help with something. He would have been done that much faster and who knows, he might not even have been in the building when whoever it was who killed him got into his office."

An annoyed look flashed across Whit's handsome, rugged features. "You can reconstruct the scenario a hundred different ways and torture yourself from now until doomsday, it still won't change anything. Still won't bring my father back," he emphasized. "Why don't you put that energy to better use and make sure that his company continues to operate and thrive?"

If she was going to devote herself to something, it shouldn't be work as usual. At least not yet, Elizabeth thought.

"What about catching his killer?" she wanted to know.

Whit swallowed an expletive. The last thing he wanted her to do was attempt to track down a killer. "That's what the police are for."

Elizabeth turned to look at him again, taking in the hard ridges of his profile. Analyzing what he had just said.

"Yes, but you don't believe that," she guessed. She saw a muscle in his cheek flicker slightly. She was right, she congratulated herself. "You think that vengeance belongs to you."

Whit stopped his sports car just within the entrance of AdAir Corp's parking facility and looked around. Her car was all the way over to the left, near the rear elevator. Getting his bearings, he drove straight for the vehicle.

Bringing the car to a stop beside Elizabeth's vehicle, Whit turned to look at the woman who had already caused him to lose control once. With effort, he pushed that whole episode behind him.

"You sure you're up to driving home?" he asked. His tone made it sound like a routine question instead of one fueled by genuine concern—which it was.

Whit was keeping a very tight rein on himself, fearing that if he allowed even a glimmer of emotion to come through, everything would be lost because the dam would most certainly give way and break apart. He was not about to allow that to happen.

"I'm sure," she told him, then smiled as she added, "thanks for asking."

Whit shrugged, not knowing how to respond to her expression of gratitude. It wasn't an emotion he was accustomed to.

"I don't want to have to identify your body, too," he told her matter-of-factly.

Elizabeth nodded, expecting nothing more from him. He was very tightly wound right now, she thought, more than willing to give him a pass. The fact that she always did, no matter what the transgression, wasn't something she was about to dwell on.

"You won't have to," she promised.

Getting out of his car, Elizabeth crossed to her own, taking careful, small steps as if she was afraid that tilting even a fraction of an inch in any direction would send her sprawling to the ground. Discovering her boss's body the way she had had thrown her equilibrium into complete turmoil and she found herself both nauseous and dizzy.

Or maybe that was due to the tiny human being she was carrying within her.

In either case, she couldn't allow herself to display any signs of weakness—especially around Whit.

At the last moment, just before she got into her car, Elizabeth turned and looked in his direction. Whit was still watching her, as if he wasn't entirely certain that she was capable of navigating either herself or her vehicle once she got behind the wheel.

"If you need to talk—about anything at all," she emphasized, "call me. You have my number."

Actually, he didn't, Whit thought. He had deliberately deleted it from his contact list the morning after they'd slept together. He had done it predominantly to remove immediate temptation from his reach. But in actuality it had been a token gesture to assuage his conscience, since obtaining Elizabeth's phone number again would have taken almost no effort whatsoever on his part. All he had to do was pull it out of her personnel file.

So far, he had resisted the temptation to do so.

Not wanting to prolong this exchange between them a second longer than he had to—because it might lead to results he told himself he shouldn't allow to happen—Whit said, "Yes, I do."

"And you'll call if you need to talk?" she asked, watching his expression.

"I won't need to talk," Whit told her flatly.

Someone else might have been rebuffed, gotten into their car and driven away. But that someone else wasn't Elizabeth. Then again, no one else would have had her motivation and desire to be there for Whit.

"But if you do," she emphasized, looking at him intently.

Whit nodded, surrendering because he wanted to finally bring this to a close. "Yes, I'll call," he agreed. With that, he slammed the driver's side door closed.

He wouldn't call, Elizabeth thought, sliding in behind the steering wheel of her vehicle. She closed the door and tugged her seat belt from behind her, clicking it into place.

The man could be unbelievably stubborn, Elizabeth thought, but there was absolutely nothing she could do about that.

Nothing she could do about any of it, except to

express her heartfelt sorrow and regret. That and be there if Whit discovered that he did need someone to turn to.

She knew for a fact that Whit's work kept him so busy he had no close friends to share things with. And if he had ever been close to his younger siblings, Carson and Landry, the past few years had seen those relationships drifting apart. Carson had enlisted in the Marines several years ago and from what she had heard, Landry had been taken over by Patsy, her mother, who was grooming the girl for a "suitable marriage" with someone the woman viewed as the "right" son-in-law.

Whit had thrown himself completely into his work for the sole purpose of earning his father's gratitude as well as his admiration, both of which were now off the table. Permanently.

If Reginald Adair had been proud of his firstborn, he'd never given any verbal indication of that. For the most part, the man had been distant from his family.

Elizabeth shook her head, remembering. Reginald Adair had been closer to her than he had been to his own flesh and blood, she thought now as she drove the familiar path to her town house from AdAir Corp.

You can't exactly throw rocks, now can you? Elizabeth thought, mocking herself. Talk about all work and no play—she was practically the poster girl for that cliché. All she did was work. In all honesty, she was surprised that the route from the AdAir Corp building to her home wasn't delineated with well-worn tire marks.

Except for that recent business trip she'd made with Whit to Nevada, almost all of her time was spent either at work, *going* to work or *preparing* to go to work. The drive home was usually a tired blur.

And those hours that she had put in, she thought as she drove home now, had all involved Reginald Adair. What was going to happen to her now that he was gone?

The company was far too large to shut down. Besides, it was considered the leader in its field and it was just a matter of time before it surpassed the competition. Would Whit take over the corporation? Would he just pick up where his father had left off and act as if it was all only business as usual?

His manner just now indicated that most likely he would, but the man wasn't a robot or an android. He was going to have to make time to grieve over his loss. If he didn't, eventually, it would catch up to him, causing him to break down, perhaps on a grand scale.

A scale from which there would be no way to come back. It wasn't as if things like that never happened—they did, and careers ended because of it.

Whit was too good at his job to allow that to happen, she told herself. But she was still uneasy. After all, Whit was a man, not a machine.

She had to find a way to make sure that didn't happen. For his sake as well as for the memory of Reginald Adair.

Just missing a light, she sighed and stepped on the brake. Waiting for the light to turn green, she pressed the flat of her hand against her abdomen. Her thoughts turned to the small passenger she carried there.

"I'm going to have to hold off introducing the idea of you to the world a little longer," she murmured to her stomach. "You understand, don't you? Your dad just isn't ready to hear that he created you right now, sweetie. We'll tell him when the time is right, okay?"

Elizabeth didn't bother saying out loud that the time might never be right. That was something she was going to have to deal with later, but not now.

For now, she was just going to have to put that problem on the back burner. This was absolutely *not* the time to tell Whit that their one night together had produced a dividend. She was certain that would throw him for a loop, especially at a time like this. Whit deserved to know that he was going to be a father and she had every intention of telling him—when she felt the time was right. In short, he needed to know, but not now.

Perhaps not until after it was all behind them, Elizabeth thought.

What she was afraid of was that Whit might think that she had deliberately allowed this to happen in order to trap him. Nothing could have been further from the truth. Under no circumstances did she want Whit thinking that she wanted anything from him.

In reality, she actually did want something from Whit, but it had nothing to do with the baby—or at least, not directly. She would have loved nothing better than to have Whit tell her that he wanted to marry her—but she wanted him to marry her because he wanted her and he loved her, not because he felt a sense of obligation, or because he wanted to give the baby his last name.

The last thing in the world she wanted was to look back someday and have Whit accuse her of tricking him into marrying her.

She would rather die first than have that happen to her.

To them.

And there was even a worse scenario than the one she wanted no part of. What if she told him that their one night of indescribable passion had yielded a baby and he went on to deny that the baby was his? Too busy working to form any personal relationships, she hadn't been with anyone else in a number of years.

The child she was carrying below her heart most definitely belonged to Whit Adair.

If she heard Whit deny it—or tell her to simply "take care of the problem"—it would absolutely break her heart. Not just that, but it would completely destroy the way she thought of Whit.

No, this was most definitely *not* the time to tell Whit Adair that he was going to become a father.

Perhaps, Elizabeth thought as she turned her vehicle in to her neighborhood, there would never be a right time and this would just be a secret she would keep from Whit forever.

Better that than to have her heart destroyed.

Elizabeth blew out a long, ragged breath. No matter how she looked at it, this was going to be a no-win situation.

Getting out of her car, she headed straight for the front door of her two-bedroom town house. She wanted the solace of having familiar things around her.

Preoccupied, she didn't notice the person who remained in the shadows.

The person who had followed her and was intently watching her every move.

It was hard remaining in the shadows, hard not to give in to the surge of adrenaline the observer could feel coursing through their veins, bringing with it a desire to act. A desire to have Elizabeth Shelton done away with and have her join her dead boss in whatever hell was reserved for godless people like that.

Soon. The word shimmered seductively in the observer's mind. Soon the world would be rid of the girl just like it was now rid of that pompous ass with his phony, shallow smile.

Checking the impulse to follow Elizabeth into her town house and bring her to her knees, having the so-called "administrative assistant" beg for her life, the person cleaving to the shadows savored the deed that still lay ahead. The mistake would be improved on. Adair was allowed to die too quickly. Next time, there would be torture. Slow, painful torture.

The observer smiled in anticipation.

And made plans.

As she opened the medicine cabinet to reach for the light cologne she liked to spray on before she left the house, she saw that it wasn't in its usual place. It wasn't there at all.

What had she done with it, Elizabeth asked herself, trying to remember when she'd had it last. This was getting very annoying, she thought. Yesterday, her lipstick had been missing—she never had found it.

Opening the drawer where she kept several different brushes that she used to style her hair, she saw that the cologne was lying on its side—the drawer was long and shallow. She took it out, hit the spray quickly twice and then put it back in its customary place.

What was going on with her? she thought. She was too young to be going senile.

If she was going to be of any use to Whit, she was going to have to get ahold of herself and pay attention to what she was doing, she silently upbraided herself.

Opening another drawer, she took out her spare lipstick and put it on. At least that was where it was supposed to be, she thought with some measure of relief.

Chapter 4

Ordinarily, unless he was busy with something that necessitated his coming into work on the weekend, Friday night was the time Whit left the city for the family ranch. Adair Acres had initially been an investment property that his father had bought with the very first million he ever made.

Totaling more than 180 acres, the sprawling ranch, comprised of alfalfa fields and avocado groves to name just a couple of its crops, was located halfway between Carlsbad and Fallbrook and was also within easy driving distance of San Diego and AdAir Corp.

The ranch was also not far from Los Angeles.

The location had been chosen in part to placate his mother, Patsy, who hated the country and thrived in more social surroundings. In years past, she'd made it her mission to turn the ranch into a show-place that people craved an invitation to visit.

For Whit, the ranch represented happier times. It was where he had grown up and where he now went to find inner peace. It was his escape from the world when the world became too demanding. Working on the ranch always seemed to calm him. It helped him cope with whatever demands he had to face come Monday morning.

Not that he was exactly out in the wilderness. Adair Acres came with a twelve-thousand-square-foot hacienda-style house that had seven bedrooms and eight and a half bathrooms. He still had a room there, as did Carson and Landry. His parents had separate suites as well, on opposite sides of the ha-cienda. As far as Whit was concerned, the ranch would always be home to him.

But this weekend, because of what had hap-pened, Whit opted to remain in the San Diego bungalow he maintained during the week, located only a few minutes away from work. While the ranch was his haven, he wanted to be available to the local police should any progress be made in his father's murder investigation. He wanted to be of any help he possibly could.

So far, he hadn't heard a word. Maybe the police was too busy breaking the news to his family, Whit thought. Maybe it made him a coward, but he was relieved that he didn't have to be the one to tell his brother and sister about the murder. Especially his sister.

Both his personal cell phone and the landline he maintained remained frustratingly silent as far as getting a call from the police detective handling his father's case went.

Oh, both phones rang almost incessantly, but each call that came in was either from someone expressing their sincere sympathies, or from someone who was associated with some venue of the media. Those callers were looking for exclusive details that hadn't been broadcast by every other form of media that was covering his father's horrific murder.

Whit hadn't wanted to turn off his phones because that meant he would also miss the legitimate calls, coming from his family or his father's friends. But it got to the point that having the phones on became unbearable. He dealt with the problem the only way he knew how—he shut off the phones after he'd called everyone he felt he needed to inform of his father's untimely death.

In a great many of the cases, he found that he didn't have to bother with the notification. The people he called were already informed, either via the news or because they had received a call from Elizabeth. A few of the people she'd called told Whit that she had broken the news to them as gently as possible, saying she'd felt that they would want to be told personally rather than hearing about it from one of the various news programs. Thinking that he was behind this, they'd thanked him for her call.

About to set the record straight, Whit decided just to let things stand. It was easier that way.

She was efficient, he'd give her that, Whit thought as he hung up for the last time and turned off his landline. At first glance, Elizabeth Shelton had struck him as a frail, delicate hothouse flower. But as he grew to know her, he'd realized it was a case of her being more of an iron butterfly than an orchid. He had seen her tackle all manner of things head-on without any hesitation.

But that still didn't keep him from feeling as if he needed to protect her.

Maybe, he mused, it was because that gave him something to focus on other than the details of the terrible occurrence that kept exploding into his consciousness just when he thought he had a handle on the way he felt.

Just when he thought he could deal with his father's death, it sneaked up on him and erupted in his brain all over again.

Unable to sleep more than a few minutes at a time, Whit finally gave up at around five in the morning. Instead of tossing and turning, he decided to start making lists of things that had to be attended to either immediately or somewhere down the line.

First and foremost, he had to make the funeral arrangements. His father's body still hadn't been released from the coroner's office, but he had put the family lawyer, Nathan Miller, on that. He'd told Miller to use his influence—and whatever else was necessary—to move his father's autopsy to the front of the line.

Quite frankly, Whit didn't see why there even had to *be* an autopsy, since the cause of his father's death was obvious: it was a death by bullet straight to the heart. He felt the medical examiner could just dig the bullet out of his father's chest, allowing them to learn what caliber gun had been used. What else was there to learn about the crime?

But nothing, Whit had come to learn, was ever as simple as it seemed to be. So he'd told Miller to do whatever he had to—pull whatever strings needed to be pulled—in order to get his father's body released.

A little after nine in the morning, his brain had temporarily placed itself on hold. He stopped writing lists, most of which were beginning to make little sense to him at this point.

Pacing around the bungalow like a caged tiger, Whit stopped dead when he felt the incessant vibration coming from his hip pocket. Unable to cut himself completely off from all communications, he'd picked up a burner phone from AdAir Corp's developmental lab early Saturday morning. He'd given the number to the family lawyer, then told the man to call him the minute he got Reginald's body released.

"Hello?" Whit practically shouted even before he held the phone to his ear.

Miller didn't bother to give his name. He assumed the burner phone had caller ID. "I finally got the ME to release your father's body a few minutes ago. Where do you want it sent?"

Now there was a sentence he'd never thought he'd have to answer, Whit thought. He rattled off the address of the funeral parlor he'd hired to handle all the arrangements regarding his father's funeral. A few discreet inquiries had convinced him that he could trust the almost 150-year-old establishment not to turn the proceedings into a media circus—or, at the very worst, not add to it.

"Got it," Nathan Miller said. "Do you want me to release a statement regarding viewing your father's body lying in state?"

"He's not going to be lying in state and there's not going to be any viewing of the body," Whit snapped. "Just a funeral. Cut-and-dried," he said, as if that was to be the final word.

Except that it wasn't. Some flexibility was

called for. "You might want to think about that, sir," Miller advised. "We don't want anyone to think that you've got something to hide."

Whit frowned at the phone. "Not that I give a damn what anyone thinks, but exactly why would they believe that?"

"If you rush this, that's the natural assumption that people will make," Miller explained patiently, "that you don't want something to be seen, to be taken into account. Your father was murdered suddenly. Don't let him be buried the same way. He was a great man, Whit," Miller reminded him.

Obviously, he was going to have to okay a viewing. Something else that was apparently out of his control, Whit thought.

"Okay," he agreed reluctantly, "one day."

"Two or three would be better," Miller pointed out quietly.

Even one day was more than he wanted. He didn't want to share his father with the world. He just wanted to be able to bury the man in peace.

"One day," Whit repeated more firmly.

"One day," the voice on the other end of the line echoed, giving in.

"Call me on this line when the funeral parlor has my father's body," Whit instructed. He terminated the call before Miller could agree.

Whit had no sooner placed the burner phone back in his pocket than his front doorbell rang.

His entire six-foot-two body stiffened as every fiber within him automatically went on high alert. He had specifically chosen this bungalow for its privacy and relative inaccessibility to the public. Overlooking the ocean, the two-bedroom abode was situated within a gated community. Access was difficult at best, but he was not about to underestimate the ingenuity of enterprising, relentless reporters and bloggers.

He was, however, determined to ignore the intrusion. Whit remained unresponsive to the doorbell, planning to wait out the invader until he or she gave up and went away.

But after whoever was on the other side of the door had rung the bell two separate times, he suddenly heard a female voice call out, "Mr. Adair, please open the door. It's Elizabeth Shelton."

Surprised, he strode quickly to the door, punched in the security code to disarm the system and then flipped the two locks he had installed himself—just in case.

Pulling open the door, he found that Elizabeth was indeed on his doorstep. She was still pale, but she looked a great deal better now that she wasn't wearing blood-soaked clothes.

"What are you doing here?" Whit asked her as he opened the door wider.

"I came to check on you," Elizabeth told him

simply. Then, to take the strictly personal edge off, she added, "Your father would have wanted me to."

"No, he wouldn't," Whit contradicted. "My father didn't concern himself with things like that. At least not to my knowledge," he qualified. This past year or so, he had a feeling that Elizabeth had probably been closer to the old man than he was.

Still standing on the other side of the threshold, Elizabeth asked politely, "May I come in?"

Whit lifted his shoulders in a careless, noncommittal shrug and stepped over to one side.

"You might as well," he replied.

It was only after she came in and he had closed the door behind her, rearming the security system, that he noticed the brown bag she was carrying. He couldn't quite place the aroma coming from it.

"What's that?" Whit asked, nodding at the take-out bag.

"I had a feeling that you probably haven't had anything to eat yet," Elizabeth told him.

She put the large bag down on the nearest flat surface. In this case, it was a highly polished ebony coffee table. At the last moment, she slid a magazine on the table under the bag.

Whit looked at the bag but made no move to open it or look inside. Eating was not a priority for him at the moment.

"It's Thai food," she told him as if he had asked what she'd brought. "You seemed to really like that Thai restaurant outside the hotel in Nevada," she reminded him, referring to their fateful business trip.

That night, with his inhibitions and restraints loosened, he would have liked a serving of dirt as long as they were sharing it together, Whit thought. But he kept that to himself and merely nodded at her comment.

"Thanks," he murmured, still making no effort to open the bag and take out its contents.

It wasn't her place to tell him what to do and she knew it. But at the same time, she wasn't about to leave until he made some sort of an effort to eat *something*.

"It only does you some good if you actually take it out and eat it," she coaxed.

Whit still made no move to open the brown bag.

Okay, if he wasn't going to open up the bag and take the food out, Elizabeth thought, making up her mind, she was going to dish it out for him.

Not wanting to just walk into the kitchen and begin rummaging through his cabinets like some unchecked, nosy neighbor, she asked Whit, "Where do you keep your plates and silverware?"

He was still processing the fact that she had taken it upon herself to come here. Coming to, he indicated the cabinet right behind Elizabeth. It was to the left of the sink.

"Right there," he said. Expressionless, he continued to look at her.

Elizabeth walked over to the cabinet he'd just indicated and opened the door to find a stack of medium-size plates.

"How are you holding up?" she asked, taking what she needed. Her back was to him.

The question seemed to come out of left field. "What?"

Plate in hand, she took several utensils out of the drawer and put them down on the counter. She began emptying the bag. There were four containers in all.

"How are you holding up?" she repeated, dispensing a little from each container onto his plate, then moving it and the necessary utensils in front of him.

"Fine," he all but bit off. "I'm holding up just fine. How are you holding up?"

"Still trying to process it," she admitted honestly, making him ashamed for having snapped the answer at her. "I keep waiting for your father to call me on the phone and say that a mistake had been made. That he's fine and did I remember that the presentation I'm making for him is at eight on Monday."

The smile on her lips was one of the saddest Whit could ever recall seeing.

"I can't really believe he's gone," she told him

quietly. Taking a breath, she asked him, "Have you heard from the police yet?"

Her question instantly alerted him. "No, why? Have you? Is there any news?"

But Elizabeth could only shake her head. "Not that I know of. But then, I really don't expect them to tell me anything. I thought that if they found anything at all, you'd be the one they'd tell."

Whit shook his head. "I haven't heard a word." Since Elizabeth had put herself out like this, he felt he owed it to her to let her know the little bit of progress that *had* been made. "What I do know is that the coroner released my father's body."

Saying those words felt so surreal, he thought. Right up to the end, his father had always been in such excellent physical shape. Reginald Adair seemed to be larger-than-life and up to any challenge. Reducing him to just a body, an empty shell, felt so very wrong, and yet that was all his father was now—a body waiting to be interred.

The very thought was painful to deal with.

"Oh." Elizabeth had just assumed that the autopsy would take longer. But now that Mr. Adair's body had been released, there were things that required immediate attention. "Would you like me to handle the funeral arrangements for you?" she asked. It wasn't something she would have welcomed doing, but she wanted to take the burden away from him and lighten his load if that was at all possible. It was the least she could do for him at a time like this.

"That's already taken care of," he told her, then belatedly, because he knew she was trying her best to help, he added, "Thank you."

"Nothing to thank me for," she replied. "I didn't do anything."

"But you were willing to," he countered. Whit looked at the containers that were on his counter, surrounding the now empty bag. "Would you like to stay and have some of this?" he asked, indicating the takeout she had brought.

Elizabeth had always liked Thai food herself. But right now the thought of consuming it had her stomach threatening to rebel violently even though it was still empty. Just the mere thought of food made her want to throw up. Without thinking, she pressed her hand to her stomach and shook her head.

"Thank you, but no, I'll have to take a pass on that for now."

He looked at her, remembering how much she had enjoyed the meal that night that they shouldn't have spent together. She'd eaten her portion with great appreciation. Having her pass on it now could only mean one thing. "Aren't you feeling well?" he asked her.

She suddenly realized what she was doing and immediately dropped her hand to her side.

"I think I've got a touch of stomach flu. Or maybe it's just my way of responding to Friday night. I really haven't eaten anything since it happened," she confessed. And it was true, she hadn't eaten anything except for a few crackers, and even those hadn't stayed down.

But it wasn't Reginald's murder that had her stomach in such an upheaval. The reason her stomach instantly cramped up at the mere thought of food was all due to the small passenger she was carrying around.

So far, she found herself throwing up everything that passed her lips, including water. She'd heard that it was to be expected for some women and that it wouldn't last, but that didn't really help her cope with the awful feeling she was forced to walk around with.

All her attempts to divert her attention to something else only worked for short while. And then another wave of nausea would rise up and claim her and she became absolutely miserable.

Again.

Elizabeth stepped back from the counter. She'd done what she had come to do: asked about his state of mind and gotten him to contemplate eating.

"Well, I'd better go. If you need anything, or if I can help in any way," she emphasized, "please don't hesitate giving me a call." She underscored her request by touching his arm and meeting his eyes. "At the very least, I can take care of calling everyone with the details of the funeral."

She could see by the look in his eyes that he hadn't gotten that far in his thinking yet.

"Your father touched a lot of lives during his time on earth," she reminded him. "They're all going to want to come to the funeral and pay their respects."

Whit suppressed the sigh that rose to his lips. She was right. A lot of people would want to attend the funeral. To leave them out wasn't advisable. There might be repercussions.

So much for having a small and intimate service where he could deal with his grief privately.

He nodded. "You're right," he acknowledged. "I'll be in touch later," he told her.

Maybe he would and maybe he wouldn't, she thought. But she had pushed all she could today. Ultimately, it was all up to him whether he would accept her help or not. For now, she would leave him to his thoughts.

Elizabeth flashed a quick, small smile at him, then stood before the door, waiting.

When Whit looked at her, puzzled, she told him, "You're going to have to disarm the system for me. Otherwise I can't leave. The second I try, the alarms are all going to go off and some little security person monitoring this at their desk is going to have heart failure."

It was rather a dramatic take on the matter, but essentially, she'd described the scenario that would ensue if she tried to open the door before he disarmed the system.

"Right," he agreed. "Sorry. I just assumed you knew the code."

Why would he think that? "I've never been here before, so no, I don't."

It was his turn to look puzzled. To be honest, his recollection of previous dealings was at best spotty. He was having trouble gathering his thoughts together.

"Then how did you get in through the front gate?" he wanted to know.

That had been easy. Dealing with people had never been that difficult for her as long as she thought of herself in a professional capacity. Elizabeth Shelton, private citizen, had no clout, but Elizabeth Shelton, Reginald Adair's executive assistant, could move mountains if she needed to.

"I showed the guard my AdAir Corp ID and explained why I was here. It took a little doing, but I finally convinced him."

Whit nodded. He could see her doing that. Elizabeth was the type of person who could convince anyone of anything, he thought. It was her appearance that did it. She looked far too innocent to lie.

And she never abused that ability. Whit found that admirable. He found a lot of things admirable about her, he realized.

The next moment, he blocked that thought.

Whit had taken her up on her offer to help and she began immediately. There was an endless amount of people to call, notifying them where the funeral and the reception were going to be held. Then, of course, there were also the actual arrangements that needed to be made. Caterers to be called, menus to be selected.

It began to feel as if the phone was a permanent attachment to her ear. Her arm had gotten tired, so she'd opted for a headset. It allowed her to continue with this sadness, plowing her way through so that she could finish sometime in the foreseeable future.

As she called numbers and talked to people, often repeating herself, she paced about her town house. Pausing after a call, she slipped the headset down to rest around her neck. She moved it back and forth, trying to work out a crick. A noise coming from the vicinity of her front door caught her attention.

She cocked her head, listening. She could have sworn she saw her doorknob turning ever so slightly, as if someone was attempting to get in.

"Hello? Is anyone there?" she called out.

The doorknob stopped moving.

Or maybe it had never moved to begin with and her mind was playing tricks on her.

"Face it, you've had a huge shock and you're jumpy," she lectured herself. "Calm down. There's nobody there."

But just in case, she inputted Whit's cell number. With her finger hovering over Send she approached the door and opened it quickly.

But there was no one there. With a huge sigh of relief, she closed it again and got back to work.

She missed seeing the shadow of the person who was hiding just out of sight.

Chapter 5

He hadn't been able to gather his thoughts together. Ordinarily much more eloquent on paper than he was when he spoke, this time it was as if his mind had been a chalkboard that had been washed down. Chalk left no impressions on it. And so it was with him. Numbed by this horrible event, no words came to his mind. Nothing.

As if sensing his situation, Elizabeth had offered to "help."

Help, he thought now with a suppressed dry laugh. She hadn't helped, she'd written the whole thing, somehow instinctively knowing just what it was he wanted to say and putting it down in words that, once they were written, could effectively reach everyone who had come here today.

"I don't know how to thank you," he'd told her when she'd turned over the pages to him.

"The look on your face already has," she'd replied.

He read it quickly. Every word was golden, he thought. And just like that, he was back on even keel—because of Elizabeth.

Whit stood at the podium, looking at the sea of faces before him. There were hundreds of people sitting in uncomfortable pews, waiting for him to say something that would make some sort of sense out of his father's untimely and violent departure from this world. The eulogy was right in front of him, a combination of a few hurried notes of his own and Elizabeth's rather insightful suggestions.

She was proving to be indispensable, Whit thought.

The funeral had turned out to be standing room only. The church where the service was held was filled to overflowing with his father's large extended family, plus his friends, and then there were the people who wanted or felt obligated to pay their last respects. Lastly, there were the curious, the onlookers and the people who had no lives of their own and were attracted to events that involved people of accomplishment.

His father certainly was that.

Despite the fact that everything had been hastily arranged, family members had managed to come from all over the country. Again, Elizabeth had been instrumental in helping to reach all of them. The woman truly was turning out to be far more helpful than he had ever anticipated, taking it upon herself to make sure no one was left out and that everything went as smoothly as possible.

Whit saw his father's older sisters, his aunts Emmaline and Rosalyn, seated in the row behind his mother, his brother and his sister. Rosalyn's three daughters sat next to her, while Emmaline's son, Noah, was missing—the only family member he and Elizabeth hadn't been able to reach.

His mother, Whit noted, seemed to be feeding on the attention that being Reginald Adair's grieving widow generated.

There were people throughout the gathering whose faces would have been recognizable on the news programs, both local and national, as well as people who tended to be almost invisible, moving about unnoticed by those who passed them on the street.

His father's death—especially the manner of his death—had been a jolting surprise to everyone.

Whit pushed on with the eulogy. He was almost finished.

"At sixty-two, my father seemed far too young to leave us. I was so sure that he would be around for another twenty, thirty years, by which time I'd have most—but not all—of my questions answered. Now I'm just going to have to try to channel my father whenever a particularly difficult situation comes up."

A resigned smile curved the corners of his lips. "But it certainly won't be easy. Neither will it be easy living in a world without Reginald Adair in it. But we'll have to try to find a way, because that's what he would have expected of us. I have a lot to live up to," he told the people before him. "We all do."

Finished, Whit returned to his seat. The oppressive weight he had been struggling with since he'd been told of his father's violent death seemed to have lifted just a little.

Sitting several rows behind Whit and his family, Elizabeth never took her eyes off him.

The set of his shoulders told her just how uncomfortable Whit was standing before all these people, giving the eulogy, although she doubted if anyone else was aware of it. He was good at putting on a brave, solid front.

As was she.

Caravans of dark limousines and passenger cars took the mourners from the cemetery where Reginald's body was interred to Adair Acres, a good distance away, for the reception.

Because of the suddenness and the manner of Adair's demise, the family was dealing with varying degrees of emotional distress. Elizabeth had taken it upon herself to step in and had made all the arrangements for the reception that was held after the funeral. She'd employed highly recommended caterers to handle the food and had instinctively made sure that everyone who deserved an invitation to this gathering of family, friends and associates received one.

"I'm beginning to see why Dad thought so highly of you," Whit told her when their paths crossed during the second hour of the reception.

Left to himself, Whit would have continued to go out of his way to avoid having any contact with Elizabeth, accidental or otherwise. However, his father's murder had changed everything—or rather, the way Elizabeth had pitched in and handled the thousand and one details that went into coordinating the church service, the funeral and the gathering afterward had changed everything. He couldn't ignore what she had done and how much of a burden she had taken off his shoulders by doing it.

"I don't know if I could have pulled any of this off the way you did," he confessed. "And on my own, this would have been a disaster." Facing her, he said, "Thank you for everything."

Elizabeth forced a smile to her lips. He had

no idea just what sort of feat she had pulled off, she thought. She'd done all this—handled details, hired limousines, made all the necessary adjustments to schedules—while feeling as sick as the proverbial dog.

She felt very proud of the fact that Whit would never guess that she would have given anything to just curl up in her bed and try to sleep until this constant nausea finally abated. But she didn't have that luxury, so she'd tried to get her mind off her physical misery by being nonstop busy.

For the most part, it worked.

The smile Elizabeth gave him now wasn't forced, it was one of encouragement.

"I'm sure you could have," she told Whit. "But I am glad I could help in some small way."

The past few days had been a complete strain on him and Whit felt as if he'd been sleepwalking through most of it, only intermittently aware of his surroundings. During all that he had been only peripherally aware of Elizabeth. But now, when he was able to draw a breath, thinking this was almost all behind him, he looked at Elizabeth, *really* looked at her, and it gave him a little pause. All semblance of color was gone from her face. She looked drained.

Guilt pricked at his conscience.

"Are you feeling all right, Elizabeth?" he asked.

"Yes," she answered, perhaps a bit too quickly. Then, regrouping, she asked, "Why?"

"I don't know, you look a little…pale to me," he finally said, summing up her appearance as tactfully as possible.

She knew perfectly well why she looked like a ghost searching for a final resting place, but she grasped at the all too available excuse.

"It's just the result of having to come to grips with the shock of what happened to your father," she told him. "I've never known anyone who was murdered before and since I *was* the one who found the body, it was doubly upsetting," she reminded him.

"Right."

What was he thinking, Whit silently upbraided himself. Of course, this had all been a terrible shock to her and perforce it had to be fresh in her mind, since his father had been murdered just a little more than a week earlier.

"Sorry." He was being completely insensitive, Whit realized. Besides, what woman liked having someone point out flaws in her appearance?

"Nothing to be sorry about," Elizabeth assured him. If she was being honest about it, she rather liked the fact that he had even noticed her appearance. Aside from that one night, she sincerely doubted that she'd ever been anywhere on Whit's radar. Certainly not the way he was on hers. "You were just showing your concern."

He didn't know *what* he was actually showing. But Whit did know that he didn't want Elizabeth to feel that she *had* to take on all these various obligations by herself. As he looked at her, bits and pieces of that one glorious night they had spent together came rushing back to him, almost against his will.

Suddenly, he found himself remembering all the emotions that had risen up within him when he was with her. When he was holding her in his arms. Making love with her.

Wanting her.

Seriously? You're thinking about that now, with the lieutenant governor of the state standing less than two feet away? he reprimanded himself.

The lieutenant governor wasn't the only high-ranking official who had attended the funeral. There were a couple of senators and a few congressional representatives paying their respects as well. His father, Whit couldn't help thinking, would have eaten this up happily. Except now he couldn't, Whit reminded himself with regret.

"Thanks for this," he told Elizabeth just before he went to exchange a few words with the lieutenant governor. At the moment, his mother appeared to be hanging on every one of the man's words.

His mother, he had known from a very young

age, was one incredible piece of work. Her first and foremost priority had always been herself, to the exclusion of all else.

Nothing had changed.

Whit knew that if she could have, his mother would have filled her world with high-ranking officials, well-known celebrities and philanthropists of the highest magnitude. For the moment, his father's murder and subsequent funeral played right into her hands. It gave her the perfect setting for garnering the kind of attention she thrived on.

She probably saw it as the best thing that had ever happened to her, Whit couldn't help thinking.

Bit by bit, Whit was beginning to understand why his father would spend so much time at work rather than coming home. His father and his mother were drifting apart. They had been for a long time now.

As strange as it seemed under the circumstances, he found himself feeling sorry for the man who was responsible for giving him life.

"Thank you all for coming," Nathan Miller said several days later, addressing the people gathered in his conference room.

Initially, the lawyer had thought that his office would have been a sufficient place to hold the reading of Reginald Adair's will, but given the number of people mentioned in it, the senior partner of his law firm felt the conference room would feel less crowded.

Even so, Miller had had to have extra chairs brought in beyond the ones already at the conference table to accommodate everyone.

Beyond the dramatically grieving widow and Reginald Adair's children, included were his two sisters and Rosalyn Adair Cross's three daughters, not to mention a number of faithful servants, employees and colleagues, all of whom received some sort of mention and bequest in Adair's will.

Miller, of course, was quite aware of the will's content, having drawn it up for his longtime client years ago. Just recently, they had gone over all the will's stipulations to make sure everything was up-to-date and still met with Adair's approval.

Adair's death—or more accurately, his murder, the lawyer silently amended—might have been untimely, but at least Reginald had been completely prepared for the end of his life. His will went into great detail as to the distribution of all his worldly possessions.

"Well, I think we can get started now," Whit told the lawyer. "It looks like everyone's here."

Actually, he thought, it looked as though *more* than everyone was here. He wondered if there were going to be some disappointed people by the time the reading was finished.

He hoped that this wouldn't get ugly.

Miller nodded. "Very well." Making himself as comfortable as he could under what he foresaw was going to turn out to be a rather uncomfortable occurrence, the lawyer began reading. "It begins in the standard way," he told the gathering. "'Being of sound mind and body, I, Reginald Adair…'"

The first things that were touched upon were the smaller bequests. Generous monetary awards for years of faithful services were enumerated.

Patsy frowned and shifted in her seat as each sum, and its recipient, was read aloud.

The largest of those went to Elizabeth, who seemed stunned by the amount and the very fact that she was included at all. She had come to the reading because she'd felt she might be needed—and because Miller had requested her presence. But she had assumed he meant it in some sort of professional capacity, not as an intended recipient who was mentioned in the will.

She was still dealing with her surprise as Miller informed Adair's sisters of the amounts left to each of them and their offspring.

The fact that no money was allocated to his brother, Bucannon, or his brother's children came as no surprise, since that branch of the family was exceptionally well-off. They had no need of his money.

The next paragraph, however, threw Adair's widow for a wide, dizzying loop. She stared, open-mouthed, as Miller disclosed the sizable chunk of money that was being left to Adair's first wife, Ruby—a woman who, according to Miller, had declined to be present for the reading because she felt her presence would disturb the rest of Reginald's family.

"There has to be some mistake," Patsy cried, jumping to her feet as she glared accusingly at Miller. "He wouldn't do that to me!" It was obvious that she viewed mentioning Ruby at all as a slap in the face, completely humiliating her.

Miller remained unfazed. He worded his answer as precisely as he could. "I believe he wasn't doing anything *to* you, Mrs. Adair. He was doing it *for* his ex-wife."

"No! You can't give it to her," she cried angrily. "That money doesn't belong to her."

"Apparently Mr. Adair felt that it did," Miller replied calmly. "And as you must know, I have to abide by your late husband's wishes."

Patsy's eyes blazed as she withdrew from the table in a huff. "We'll see about that!"

With that, Patsy looked as if she was about to storm out of the room. But then she sighed dramatically, murmured something about Ruby getting the money over her dead body, and sat down in her seat again.

She was obviously waiting to hear what she would continue to own once the smoke cleared.

Miller resumed with the reading as if the outburst hadn't happened.

"'Part ownership of my beloved ranch,'" the lawyer read, "'that held so many good memories for me, will go to my sister Emmaline's only son, my nephew Noah Scott.'"

That, Whit felt, had been done because Noah had enjoyed himself so much at the ranch the summers he was allowed to spend there. Those months had been the only time his aunt Emmaline would relinquish her tight hold over Noah during his adolescent years.

His mother, Whit noted, seemed to care less about the ranch. He knew she would be more than happy never to set foot on it again. Without his father around, there was no reason for her to ever have to go there again. The city, with its vibrant nightlife and all it had to offer, was far more her style.

"'And now I come to my main achievement,'" Miller read, pausing in all the places he had been instructed to pause. "'AdAir Corp. I want the company to be divided equally between all four of my children: Jackson, Whit, Carson and Landry.'"

It was as if a bomb had been dropped in all their laps.

"What?" Landry cried, confused. She looked to Whit for an explanation.

"Who's Jackson?" Carson wanted to know.

Whit's younger brother looked at his mother, waiting for an answer. Patsy in turn had turned pale for just a moment before rage took over and put color back into her face. Vivid color.

Whit felt that if there were answers to be gotten, they were going to come not from his mother's viper tongue but from his father's lawyer.

"What does he mean, *four* children? My father only had the three of us," Whit said to the man, waiting for some sort of an explanation.

But even as he said it, he could see by the look in the lawyer's eyes that he and his siblings had been under the wrong impression all these years.

"I'm afraid that's not quite accurate, Whit," Miller told him. "When your father was married to his first wife, Ruby—"

"The whore!" Patsy bit off.

Miller ignored her comment and continued as if the widow hadn't said anything.

"—they had a son they called Jackson. Jackson was kidnapped from his own garden when he was three months old. Your father did everything in his power to find Jackson, moving almost heaven and earth. But he was never able to recover the boy.

"Rightly or wrongly, your father blamed Ruby for the kidnapping. She had left the baby in the yard, unattended, for a minute while she ran in to answer the phone. When she came out, the baby was gone. Their marriage began to break down right there. Eventually, they divorced and he went on to marry your mother.

"But your father never gave up hope that his firstborn was alive and out there somewhere. Your father was absolutely convinced that Jackson would turn up someday. When he did, your father wanted him to be able to reclaim his heritage, hence the equal division of AdAir Corp's shares."

The news of another sibling joining their ranks totally floored Whit. He just wasn't sure how he was going to assimilate this latest curveball his father had sent, essentially from beyond the grave.

Trying to deal with the breadth and scope of this newest revelation, Whit looked at the lawyer. "Is there anything else that we should know about? Any other immediate family members hiding somewhere? Or some other equally shocking piece of information?"

Miller took no offense at the sarcastic tone beneath the words. "I realize that this is a lot for you to take in," the lawyer began.

"That's an understatement if I ever heard one," Whit commented.

Miller lowered his eyes to the will, as if taking refuge in what was written there and his duty to make the parties involved aware of the situation per his client's wishes.

"Perhaps, but your father wanted to be completely honest with you."

"Then he should have said something while he was still alive," Whit snapped, feeling betrayed by the man he'd held in the highest possible esteem.

"Maybe he didn't want to upset you," Elizabeth suggested gently.

Her words were met with a look of disgust. "Well, that didn't exactly work out as planned, now did it?" Whit retorted sarcastically.

The next moment, he regretted what he'd just said and especially the way he'd said it. Elizabeth was only trying to relieve the tension ricocheting through the conference room. He should not have snapped at her the way that he had.

"Sorry, I shouldn't be taking this out on you. It's just a shock to suddenly find out at my age that I have an older brother." Frustrated, he blew out a long breath.

"All of this is pretty much of a shock," Elizabeth agreed. "But we'll deal with it. *You'll* deal with it," she said pointedly. "You always do."

Chapter 6

"You have more faith in me than I do," Whit commented after a beat.

"I have justifiable faith," Elizabeth pointed out. She had known him, studied him and been drawn to him for five years. That had made her, in her opinion, pretty much an expert on the man. "You are your father's son. You'll deal with this and anything else that might come your way."

Except, perhaps, for finding out that you're going to be a father, Elizabeth thought.

But that was something that she would have to deal with later, after this newest, completely unexpected tempest died down.

Dealing with his father's murder was bad enough.

Finding out that his father had a son he'd never mentioned but obviously kept close to his heart—well, that not only threw everything off balance, it damn near pushed Whit right over the edge.

Discovering that he had a baby on the way might just break the man completely, Elizabeth thought. At the very least, she knew that she couldn't count on Whit approaching this latest twist in a calm, rational manner. Not right now.

If by some chance Whit proposed marriage because she was pregnant with his child, she would never know if he was doing it out of a sense of obligation, out of wanting to give his child his last name or any of a dozen other reasons, none of which had anything to do with the one all-important thing that mattered to her: that he did it because he loved her.

Her loving him was a foregone conclusion. She would never have lowered her guard on that wonderful rainy night if she hadn't.

Nothing had changed in that respect, except that she'd been deeply wounded the next morning when Whit had acted as if absolutely *nothing* had happened between them. But she still loved him, even though she was fairly convinced that love had never entered the picture from Whit's side.

The heart wants what the heart wants—wasn't that the way the old saying went? She was living proof that the saying was very true. She couldn't do anything to change how she felt, just as she couldn't do anything about making the man love her.

But what she *could* do was help him weather and cope with this latest storm he was facing. And she fully intended to.

Since the reading of the will had concluded, most of the people who had gathered in the firm's conference room had begun filing out, buoyed by the fact that they were leaving a little richer than when they had walked in. They were also quite stunned by this little bombshell that Reginald Adair's lawyer had dropped, mentioning a fourth, heretofore unknown, offspring.

Whit and his siblings remained, as did his mother, who still appeared to be seething over the matter of the bequest to Reginald's ex-wife.

Elizabeth also remained behind, to see if she could be of any further immediate assistance to Whit before she went back to work. She might no longer be Reginald Adair's executive assistant, but she was still an executive assistant and she knew everything that had been on the late president's schedule, as well as everything the man had wanted to attend to and accomplish at the company.

A veritable storehouse of information, Elizabeth was still a very necessary person to have on hand.

However, first and foremost, her loyalty lay

with Whit, and although she didn't say it out loud, she was prepared to be anything he needed her to be, do anything he needed her to do.

In his own way, Whit had sensed that.

His mother, however, sensed something else. She viewed the much younger woman's presence—at the funeral, at the reading of the will and especially now with just the family unit together—as an affront to her.

Her brown eyes narrowing to intense, highly critical slits, Patsy glared at Elizabeth as Whit closed the door behind the departing family members, friends and employees. Convinced that her dead husband had been cheating on her with every woman who crossed his path, she was certain that Reginald's relationship with Elizabeth went well beyond boss and executive assistant.

"You can run along now, Elizabeth," Patsy said dismissively, gesturing toward the door. "Your meal ticket's gone, so there's no reason for you to hang around any longer."

"Mother," Whit said sharply, angry and embarrassed at his mother's belittling tone.

There was no love lost between them. Patsy's relationship with her children only encompassed how society viewed them and how that reflected on her. She had never been the all-embracing, milk-and-cookies type of mother. If the woman noticed and spoke at all to her children during their childhood years, it was to criticize them.

"She has a right to be here," Whit informed her gruffly.

"As what? Your father's little plaything?" Patsy challenged hotly.

The color of Elizabeth's cheeks instantly turned a shade of crimson, not from embarrassment but from sheer anger. Hot words of denial and outrage sprang to her tongue, but she bit them back for Whit's sake. She was not about to stoop down to the woman's level.

"Mother—" Whit began again, but got no further as his mother turned on him.

"Oh, don't tell me you don't know," Patsy cried sarcastically. "Why do you think he *valued* her so much? All those late hours they spent together—are you so naive that you think they were actually *working* all that time? Hardly," Patsy jeered, the expression on her very carefully made-up face turning ugly. "I didn't say anything because I didn't want the shame of scandal to taint our name, but now your father managed to take care of that by getting himself murdered," she summed up harshly.

Whit wasn't a little boy any longer, which meant that he didn't have to put up with and be embarrassed by his mother's tantrums, outbursts and incredibly bad behavior. "Mother, you owe Ms. Shelton an apology," Whit ordered sternly.

"For what?" Patsy demanded haughtily, her hands on her subtle hips. "She was well compensated, I'm sure. What about me?" she cried in the next breath. "Why don't you tell this trollop to apologize to *me*?"

Pushing her son aside, she confronted Elizabeth, going toe-to-toe with her. The platinum blonde was shorter than Elizabeth by an inch, but her stiletto heels made up the difference.

"How about it, you hussy? Do you want to apologize to me? Or do you have a little something on the side to surprise us with, like that bimbo Ruby and her disappearing baby?"

Elizabeth had always known that her boss's wife was a jealous shrew, but she had never thought the woman would accuse her of this sort of heinous behavior. She took offense for herself as well as the man she had worked for, a man who had always treated her with the utmost respect and kindness.

The mention of a baby threw her for a loop, as well. Had Patsy somehow guessed that she was pregnant?

The next moment, Elizabeth realized that there was no way that Patsy *could* have guessed. The woman was just being nasty.

"That is enough!" Whit ordered sharply.

Stunned by his tone, Patsy stopped short, turning to glare at her son. "You're right. I've had enough. *More* than enough!"

With that, she grabbed her purse and stormed out of the conference room, slamming the door in her wake so hard, the glass shook. For a second, Whit thought it was going to crack and come raining down into the room in shards.

But, like his resolve, it held together.

"I'm sorry." Elizabeth apologized to everyone who was left in the room, but predominantly to Whit. "I should have left when I saw that my presence was agitating her like that."

"No, we're the ones who should be sorry," Whit told her, struggling to repress a whole host of emotions that had been stirred up.

"Mother had no right to talk to you that way," Carson said, speaking up for the first time. "Mother has never been a happy woman and she doesn't want anyone else to be, either."

Because his mother's behavior had been such an embarrassment to him and his siblings, Whit abruptly changed the subject. He turned his attention to the reason he and his brother and sister had remained behind—unanswered questions.

"What can you tell me about this Jackson?" he asked the lawyer.

Miller sighed. He didn't have all that much to add to the sketchy picture. "Only that your father never stopped hoping the boy would turn up.

Periodically, Mr. Adair would hire detectives to look for his son. But the trail always remained cold. Jackson was the only thing that held his first marriage together. Your father married Jackson's mother in order to give the boy his name. He didn't really know her that well. She was already pregnant when they got married," Miller explained.

The mild-mannered lawyer's words stabbed Elizabeth right through the heart.

In order to give the boy his name.

That was exactly the reason why she had decided she wasn't going to say anything to Whit about her pregnancy. With any luck and careful camouflage dressing, she might never have to. All she knew was that she wasn't going to be part of a loveless marriage, even if it was only loveless on his part—because that, to her, was the only part that counted.

"Once the boy was kidnapped," Miller concluded, "and your father blamed Ruby for that, there was nothing to hold them together."

Carson looked at the man, puzzled. "If Dad was so crazy about this baby, why didn't he just pay the kidnapper the ransom?" Carson wanted to know.

"Because there *was* no ransom. That was the odd part," Miller said, turning to look at the younger man. "No one called or left a note, demanding money. The baby just vanished from his backyard one morning when his mother ran into the house to answer the phone—and that was the end of it."

"If there was no ransom note, then maybe who-ever took Jackson just wanted a baby of their own," Elizabeth suggested.

"That was the general consensus after a while," Miller agreed. "It fueled your father's hope that his missing son was still alive," he told Reginald's three offspring.

"Why didn't he ever tell any of us?" Landry wanted to know. "And why didn't we ever hear anything about it? Wasn't this a matter of public record, given who Dad was?"

More than the others, she was particularly crushed by this revelation. She'd always believed that she and her father were close. People who were close didn't withhold secrets from each other, espe-cially secrets of this magnitude. The thought that her father had kept this from all of them—from *her*—hurt her deeply.

"He wasn't the prominent person then that he was now. My guess is that he didn't tell any of you about this because he felt somehow responsible for the kidnapping," Miller said. "And, I suspect, because he didn't want to burden any of you with the cross he bore. Your mother knew," he added.

Well, that didn't come as a surprise, Whit thought. The fact that she didn't wield it like a weapon did. "I'm surprised she didn't use it to taunt him with," Whit commented to the lawyer.

"Who knows, maybe she did," Elizabeth ventured. When Whit looked at her, she explained her theory. "You weren't around much after you left home for college. Maybe she did rub your father's nose in it."

Whit had to admit that she had a point. He'd sensed that things hadn't been right between his parents for a long while now, but he had attributed it to the fact that they had completely different interests that took them in opposite directions. His father seemed to be completely devoted to his company, leaving his mother to pursue her own devices in order to amuse herself.

For a moment, he tried to put himself in his father's place and speculated how the man must have felt having a child stolen from him, living each day not knowing where the boy was or even *if* he was alive. It had to have been horrible for him, Whit thought.

"I want you to look into hiring a private detective to find this missing brother of ours," he instructed the lawyer.

Carson looked at his brother as if he had lost his mind. "If all those other detectives came up empty over the years, what makes you think the result is going to be any different now?"

"Investigative methods have improved," Elizabeth interjected, guessing at Whit's reasoning. In his place, she would do exactly the same thing. "And a fresh pair of eyes might see something that everyone else might have missed."

"In any event," Whit concluded, "it's certainly worth a try." He turned toward the lawyer, repeating his instruction in case the man just thought he was merely talking and nothing more. "Look into that for us, would you, please?"

Miller stood a little straighter, as if silently acknowledging that Whit was the head of the family now that his father was gone. "I'll get right on it, Mr. Adair."

"One question," Elizabeth said as everyone prepared to leave the conference room. Four sets of eyes turned toward her almost in unison. "What happens to that fourth share of the business if Jackson is never found? Did Mr. Adair leave some sort of a provision for that?" she asked the lawyer.

Miller shook his head. "No, he didn't. Mr. Adair was that certain that Jackson would turn up someday." He paused for a moment, considering the situation. "He probably felt if he covered that contingency in writing, it might just become a self-fulfilling prophecy."

"So that fourth share just remains in limbo forever?" Carson asked in obvious disbelief.

There were things that could be implemented

from a legal standpoint, Whit thought, but it was far too early to go into that.

"We'll deal with that after all other avenues to locate your missing brother prove to be unproductive and a sufficient amount of time has passed," Miller promised the three heirs. "For now—" he turned to look at Whit "—thank you for allowing me to serve you."

Whit put his hand on the lawyer's shoulder—the size of his hand all but dwarfed the small man's shoulder.

"You don't have to sound so humble, Nathan. The job was yours all along. I don't believe in changing ships in the middle of an ocean cruise," Whit said kindly. "Nobody's going to be handing you your walking papers."

Miller beamed, obviously relieved even though he said to the family's new head, "I'm sure I don't know what you're referring to, sir."

"You keep telling yourself that if it makes you feel better." Whit laughed.

There would be some minor changes made to the company's infrastructure when he took over heading up AdAir Corp, but nothing drastic. He had never been one who believed in change for change's sake alone, nor did he believe in flexing his muscles just because he could. He believed in results, not showmanship.

Since Landry and Carson had arrived in Carson's car, they would drive back to the ranch to-gether. As they departed, and Miller returned to his office, that left Whit standing in the hallway with Elizabeth.

"How about you?" he asked. "Can I give you a lift back home?"

She shook her head. "Actually, I took half of a vacation day from the office so I'll be going back there now that this is over. And since I drove," she continued with a smile, "I will be providing my own ride back. But thank you for the offer."

He nodded, walking with her to the eleva-tor. Taking a deep breath, he began framing his apology. "I'd like to apologize again for what my mother said—"

She held up her hand like a traffic cop stopping the flow of vehicles.

"No need. We're not accountable for what our parents say or do. I know your mother never cared for me. I think she suspected every woman who in-teracted with your father. It was no secret that she didn't trust him," Elizabeth said, only telling him what she was sure he already knew. "Your father was a very good-looking man who prided himself on staying in shape. Even though anyone look-ing at your mother would know that she did the same—she is a very strikingly beautiful woman who takes wonderful care of herself—I suppose fear doesn't have to be rational. Your mother was afraid that someone would steal him away from her."

"No," he contradicted. "She was afraid that someone would steal his *money* away from her."

"Ah, yes, but having another, possibly younger woman steal your father away from her would, in her eyes, be the ultimate humiliation. In her mind, she might not be able to rise above it, and she held your father accountable for her feelings of inadequacy. Looking at your mother, I'd say that she was a beauty when she was younger, the kind that turned men's heads no matter what they were doing at the time.

"Sometimes," Elizabeth continued as they stepped into the elevator and Whit pressed the button for the ground floor, "women like that don't accept aging gracefully and their insecurity makes life an absolute hell for those around them. Your father talked about that to me once," she told Whit. "That your mother didn't trust him and that really wounded his pride. That's not to say that women didn't throw themselves at your father on a fairly regular basis," she emphasized. "He was tall, good-looking and wealthy. Women have broken up marriages for a great deal less."

Getting off the elevator, they both walked toward the building's entrance. "I still can't believe that we're never going to see him again," she admitted as they neared the entrance.

Whit nodded. "Me neither. I think the only reason my mother's adjusted so well to this is because she hardly ever saw him during the last five or seven years." Reaching the door, he pushed it open for her, then stepped over the threshold himself. "Well, I'll see you back in the office later," he told her, then explained just in case she was wondering, "I've got a couple of things—if not more—to tend to first."

She made a calculated guess, fairly certain that she was right. "Going to the police station?"

It was getting so that nothing she said surprised him any longer. She seemed to be completely in tune to his thinking. He supposed he should be grateful that she wasn't a mind reader—otherwise, things might really get awkward.

"I want to put some pressure on the investigating detective. There've been no further reports or updates. It feels like they've just given up looking for my father's killer. It's like they think this was a one-time crime instead of someone on a rampage. That means whoever did it isn't a threat to the average citizen."

She nodded, agreeing with him. "Well, they have that wrong. I know I won't feel safe until they find whoever did it."

It could be anyone until that person had a name, she thought. Until the killer was brought to justice, she was going to be looking over her shoulder, regarding almost everyone suspiciously. That was no way to live a life, she thought.

They parted at the front door, with Whit going toward the parking structure while Elizabeth headed toward the large aboveground parking lot.

As she walked, she picked up her pace, wanting to get back to the office before her pile of things to do became totally insurmountable.

Approaching her car, Elizabeth rummaged through her purse for her keys. Finding the fob, she pulled it out, aimed in the general direction of her vehicle and pressed the release button. Because of the distance, the sound was muffled, but she heard all four locks popping up and standing to attention.

Just as she reached her car, her keys slipped from her hand, falling to the ground. Impatient with herself, she muttered the word *klutz* under her breath as she bent down to retrieve her keys.

That was when she saw it. The tire on the driver's side was slashed.

A chill ran down her spine.

She wasn't sure just what had made her look over toward the rear passenger side tire at that moment, but she did.

It was slashed, as well.

The chill running down her spine plummeted to subzero temperatures. Holding her breath, Elizabeth circled her car, coming over to the other side.

As she walked, she looked all around the immediate area. There was no one within sight.

Gathering her courage to her, she looked down at her tires on that side of the car.

They were slashed as well.

Chapter 7

Getting into his car, Whit buckled up and was just about to turn his key in the ignition when his cell phone rang. For a moment, he debated just letting the call go to voice mail. He could always call whoever was on the other end of the line back later.

Nonetheless, habit had him glancing at the screen to see who the caller was. When he saw that it was Elizabeth, a sense of uneasiness had him hitting the green symbol on his screen. He'd just now left her. What would prompt her to call him so soon?

Something was wrong.

"Hello, Elizabeth?"

Just the sound of his voice took her racing adrenaline down a notch. Everything was going to be all right, she told herself.

"Looks like I'm going to be taking you up on that offer for a ride," Elizabeth said, doing her best to sound calm.

"Sure. I'll be right there. What changed your mind?" he wanted to know.

Elizabeth looked down at her slashed tires. "I had it changed for me."

There was a strange stillness in her voice that he didn't recognize. It almost didn't sound like her, Whit thought. "Elizabeth, is something wrong?"

She thought of just telling him everything was fine—he'd see for himself soon enough. But she saw no reason for the charade in this case. There was absolutely nothing to be gained by putting up a so-called brave front.

"You might say that," she told him, "although I could be jumping the gun."

"Because?" Whit pressed, urging her to give him a fuller explanation.

"My car was vandalized."

"You mean like someone drew graffiti on it?" And why would that make the car inoperable, he wondered.

"No, like tires slashed. All four of them," she told him in a small voice that didn't allow him to guess at her emotional reaction.

Instantly alert, Whit turned the key, bringing his car to life. "Give me your exact location. I'll be right there," he promised.

He was as good as his word, Elizabeth thought. She could hear the sound of his car approaching even before she hit the button on her phone terminating the call.

His car came to a screeching stop right next to her. Whit jumped out of his vehicle, his eyes riveted on the condition of the two tires that were on his side of her car.

His first concern, though, was Elizabeth.

"Are you all right?" he wanted to know, his eyes sweeping over her to assess her state for himself.

Elizabeth gave a half shrug. She honestly couldn't say *what* she was at the moment. "As all right as I can be with four slashed tires," she answered.

He'd never heard her being flippant before, but then, these weren't exactly ordinary circumstances she was involved with, either.

"No, I mean, you aren't hurt or anything like that, are you?"

Elizabeth shook her head. "The tires were already slashed when I came out," she told Whit. "I never saw who did it." Pausing, she told him what she was considering. "You don't think this is just an odd coincidence, do you? A random prank by some stupid kid flexing his would-be tough-guy muscles for his friends or his girlfriend?" she suggested, mentally crossing her fingers that it wasn't any more than that.

But Whit shook his head, shooting down her fragile theory. "I think it's more serious than that."

She was afraid of that, Elizabeth thought, resigning herself to possibly being in someone's crosshairs. "You're talking about your father's killer, aren't you?"

Whit circled the car again, this time more slowly, checking it out just in case there was something they might have both missed seeing.

"Yes, I am."

"But why?" she wanted to know. "It doesn't make any sense, does it?"

"It doesn't have to make sense to us. The killer is the only one who counts in this scenario," Whit told her grimly. "Maybe he thinks you saw him before he pulled his vanishing act and he's afraid you're going to identify him as my father's killer to the police."

The very idea left Elizabeth numb. She struggled to get her mind in gear.

"You really think so?" she asked. It seemed to her that there was a rather large hole in that theory. "Because if I had seen the person who killed your father, I would have already identified him for the police and the killer would have been arrested, or at the very least found himself the subject of a massive interstate manhunt. Doesn't he realize that?"

Whit didn't care about the way the killer thought—he only cared about keeping Elizabeth safe.

"I don't know what the killer realizes or doesn't realize. For all we know, he might have an entirely different reason for trying to eliminate you."

Well, that certainly didn't make her feel any better, Elizabeth thought.

As he was talking, Whit got down on his knees beside the car, then crouched lower, looking at the vehicle's undercarriage.

"What are you doing?" Elizabeth wanted to know as she watched him.

Whit flattened himself as much as he could to get a good look. "I'm checking to see if whoever slashed your tires also planted an explosive device to the underside of your car."

That hadn't even occurred to her until he mentioned it. Now that he had, she couldn't understand why she hadn't thought of that herself. Her boss's killer certainly had no regard for human life. Slashed tires were a warning. A bomb would have been an execution, pure and simple.

"You actually think he planted a bomb?" she cried, feeling overwhelmed.

"Anything's possible," he replied, scanning the complete undercarriage of her disabled car one more time. It appeared clean. "I don't see any-thing," Whit told her. He rose to his feet, brush-ing some of the dirt off his trousers. Not all of it came off. With a shrug, he ignored it.

"Maybe it *is* a prank," Elizabeth said hopefully, raising that theory again.

Whit looked at her, a skeptical expression on his face. "You believe in coincidences?"

The way he asked told her his opinion on the matter. Still, she tried to hold fast to the quickly weakening theory.

"Sometimes," she replied.

"Well, I don't," Whit answered firmly. "I think you're in danger," he told her, doing his best to keep his voice calm in order not to alarm her any more than was absolutely necessary.

Not that he saw her as a woman who panicked easily. In his opinion, if Elizabeth was able to hold it together after finding his father's body the way she had, he figured that meant that she was pretty much unflappable.

Even so, everyone had their breaking point— not to mention that she was, after all, vulnerable, and he didn't want to see anything happening to Elizabeth, for a whole host of reasons.

"What kind of danger?" she asked him quietly, wary of the answer.

"The kind of danger that involves death," Whit told her crisply. He didn't want to frighten her, but at the same time, he didn't want her thinking she was safe if she wasn't. And in his opinion, she wasn't.

She wanted him to spell it out, to spare her nothing. She needed to know what she was up against, no fancy words, no quick footwork. She wanted the truth.

"You think someone wants to kill me?"

"I sure as hell don't want you moving around like some kind of a walking target just to find out if I'm right or not."

"I can't go into hiding if that's what you're talking about." The very thought was claustrophobic to her, making it suddenly hard to breathe. She needed to be out in the open, to be accessible at any time.

He wasn't about to let her talk her way out of this. Her life could very well depend on it. "Yes, you can, and you will."

She tried to make him understand why that was impossible. "Your father's gone. There's all sorts of work to get done in his absence," she insisted.

Whit looked at her pointedly. He'd had no idea she could be *this* stubborn. "To my recollection, corpses don't get very much accomplished."

Elizabeth stared at him, stunned. "You really believe that?"

He wasn't sure what she was asking. "What?

That corpses don't get very much accomplished? Absolutely," he guaranteed.

"No," she said impatiently, waving away his response, "that someone's out to kill me."

The short answer was *yes*. He gave her the benefit of the long one instead. "I know that I don't want to be standing around twiddling my thumbs with you exposed just to find out if I'm right. My father's killer is still roaming around out there and if nothing else, we need to take preventative measures."

"That doesn't mean going into hiding," Elizabeth protested. She was beginning to get the sinking feeling that nothing she said here mattered. He was going to force her to do what he felt was best. But she felt she at least had to go on the record as being against this forced retreat to who knew where.

"I'm afraid that this time that's *exactly* what it means. And yes, you're very important to AdAir Corp, but as I've already stated, you'll do absolutely no one any good if you're dead."

"But—"

She could argue until every last one of the proverbial cows came home, but he wasn't about to let her win this one. "Don't argue with me, Elizabeth. If it helps you to go along with this, just think of it as making my father happy. He wouldn't have wanted anything to happen to you, especially not on account of him."

She didn't like it. Didn't like contemplating being inactive when working was what was helping her cope with everything at the moment. It was her way of holding herself together during this unspeakable tragedy.

But she supposed that Whit was right. She wasn't going to do anyone, or AdAir Corp, any good if she was dead.

"Remember," Whit cautioned her, "he who fights and runs away lives to fight another day."

"Like Robin Hood?" she questioned, vaguely remembering that the line was applicable to the mythical outlaw who robbed from the rich and gave to the poor—and drove Prince John absolutely crazy.

"Whatever works for you," Whit said with a dry laugh. The next moment, he was calling 9-1-1 on his cell phone, reporting the crime and then asking to be transferred to Detective Kramer in Homicide.

Detective Kramer had struck him as being rather lax about the whole investigation, but he knew it would be difficult to get another detective assigned to the case without lodging a major complaint. He wasn't ready to step on any toes just yet.

"Hello, Detective?" Whit said when he heard the phone being picked up after several moments of dead air had gone by. "This is Whit Adair—"

He heard the man on the other end sigh before he began speaking. "Sorry to tell you that there's nothing new in the investigation of your father's murder, Mr. Adair—"

"I might have something for you along those lines," Whit said, cutting the man short.

"What kind of something?" the detective asked warily.

"My father's executive assistant just found all four of her tires slashed in the parking lot of a law firm's building."

Whit could almost envision the detective coming alive.

"Give me your location," the man instructed. "I'll be right there."

Kramer's version of right there turned out to be showing up some forty minutes later. Elizabeth had just about given up and was contemplating calling a tow truck to take her car to the local tire store she dealt with when the detective finally arrived.

Getting out of his rather well-maintained vehicle, he muttered an apology. "Sorry. Traffic."

Whit looked at him, puzzled by the excuse. "I thought traffic didn't apply to the police department. Isn't that why you have sirens, to clear away the impeding vehicles?"

It was obvious that after almost two decades with the department, Kramer didn't like to be questioned. "Sirens don't do any good if there isn't a path, or some kind of a hole to drive through. It was completely bottled up." His tone said that was the end of the discussion on the subject. "So what do we have here?" he asked, looking at Elizabeth's car.

"I think it's pretty self-evident, don't you?" Whit asked.

Kramer frowned. Whether it was in response to Whit's question or because he was contemplating the vehicle was unclear.

"And you think this is somehow connected to your father's murder?" Kramer questioned.

Whit answered the question with a question of his own. "Don't you? After all, she was his assistant and she was the one who found my father's body," Whit pointed out.

Kramer inclined his head as if agreeing with him and yet not agreeing at the same time. It was obvious that he was reluctant to expand the investigation.

"Sometimes a rotten prank is just a rotten prank," he said.

"So you *don't* think someone's deliberately sending me a warning of some sort?" Elizabeth asked. All things considered, she would rather go along with the detective's theory than with Whit's. It was less unnerving that way. Even so, she had a feeling that Whit was the one who was right.

"I didn't say that," Kramer qualified.

She wanted to nail the man down. Waffling might work for the detective, but it certainly did nothing for her peace of mind.

"Then you *do* think someone's trying to tell me something, warn me about something?"

Kramer took out a small, weather-beaten notebook and made a couple of notes to himself. He used a pencil, preferring the old ways to the way the wet-behind-the-ears detectives did things these days.

"It's very possible," he replied, obviously preoccupied.

"Tell me, Detective, do you ever get splinters, sitting on the fence like that?" Whit asked him.

Because Adair came from money, losing his temper with the younger man was not an option. So Kramer replied evenly, "Just trying to stay open-minded. I'll give CSI a call to get them down here and then I'll take down your statement," the detective informed the couple, summarizing standard procedure.

With that, he turned away from them as he made his call.

"After this is over," Whit said to her, keeping his voice low, "and he goes back to the precinct, you're coming with me."

"To the office?" Elizabeth asked, assuming that he was talking about where he was heading next.

They could still get in a number of solid hours' worth of work.

"No," he told her, "to the ranch."

She didn't understand. Why was he suggesting that? "What's at the ranch?" she asked.

Had he forgotten to get something from there? She knew he spent his weekends there for the most part and that because of everything that was going on lately, his life had been thrown off balance. But even if he was going to the ranch, there was no reason to take her with him. Oh, she could think of one reason, but he had made it perfectly clear by ignoring the whole incident that there was nothing between them on that score. Hence taking her to the ranch made no sense to her.

"Safety," Whit answered.

It still wasn't making sense to her, although the uneasy feeling she'd experienced earlier was back. "I don't—"

Glancing to see if the detective was still busy— he was—Whit spelled it out for her. "Look, you can't go home because my father's killer probably knows exactly where you live and if it's all the same to you, I don't want to give him a second crack at doing you some kind of harm. The next time around," he told her bluntly, "it might not just be tires that are slashed."

She wanted to tell him he was wrong, that he was letting his imagination run away with him—

but in all honesty, she couldn't. Because the opposite might very well be true.

"I think you might be right about the killer knowing where I live," she admitted.

Immediately alert, Whit pressed her for an explanation. "Why would you think that? What haven't you told me?"

It was on the tip of her tongue to ask when he had become her keeper, but that was antagonistic and she didn't want to engage him in a clash of wills, certainly not while she was carrying his baby.

So she told him, "I thought I was imagining it, but last night, when I came home to the town house, I could have sworn that some of my things had been moved around, like someone had gone through them and then tried their very best to put everything back exactly where they'd been—except that in a couple of places, they didn't succeed."

Whit felt a surge of anger, but he managed to bank it down again. Losing his temper wasn't going to accomplish anything.

"Why didn't you call me about it?"

"Because you were already dealing with enough things and besides, I thought that maybe I was just being overly tired and imagining things. Especially since I didn't find anything missing—except for a lipstick case. But again, I just might have misplaced it. Besides, what kind of homicidal maniac steals a woman's lipstick case? That doesn't even make a good souvenir."

"I don't know," Whit answered, frustrated and exasperated with both himself and what was going on. He didn't like not being in control of things. "Maybe this guy didn't read the homicidal maniac's handbook on proper procedure and doesn't know what makes a good souvenir and what doesn't."

The next moment, Kramer was terminating his call and turning his attention back to them.

"All right, let's get that statement, shall we?" he said.

"Sure." It couldn't be soon enough for her. Half the day was gone and she hadn't accomplished most of the things she had put down on her list. She was going to have to work twice as hard to catch up, Elizabeth thought as she and Whit followed the detective to a less well-traveled area.

Any place, she thought, was preferable to going down to the precinct again.

Chapter 8

In comparison to the kind of intense questioning she had been subjected to when she had discovered Reginald Adair's body, the statement Elizabeth wound up giving to the detective this time around turned out to be extremely brief. Kramer seemed to only want the sketchiest of details.

Whit's statement required even less time to take down.

"I think I have everything I need right now," Kramer told the pair, closing the notebook he'd been writing in. He tucked it back into the inside pocket of his worn navy blue jacket. "Your contact numbers in case I have other questions are still the same, right?" he asked, looking from Whit to Elizabeth for some sort of cursory confirmation.

"Considering it's only been a little more than a week, yes, the contact numbers are still the same," Whit said, answering for both of them as he leaned against his car. He noted the look of discomfort on Elizabeth's face. His guess was that she didn't really care for Kramer and she just wanted to have this be over with. He certainly couldn't blame her.

"Very good, then," Kramer said, nodding more to himself than to either one of the people he had just questioned. And then he added a rather lofty "I'll be in touch."

With that, the detective made his way over to the forensic team. The two people who had answered the call were busy taping off this latest crime scene.

"I won't hold my breath," Whit said quietly, sharing his remark with Elizabeth.

Seeing that the detective was now engaged in what appeared to be a terse conversation with one of the crime scene investigators, Whit straightened up and looked at Elizabeth. It was time to leave.

"All right, do you want to swing by your place?" Whit asked her. When she looked at him, a puzzled expression slipping over her features, he said, "To pick up some of your things. I'm not sure how long a stay this is going to have to be."

Ideally, it would only be until his father's killer

was caught, but seeing the lax way the investigation was being conducted, he wasn't holding out much hope that the situation was going to be resolved soon.

"What things, what stay?" Elizabeth asked, confused. And then the conversation she'd had with Whit before the detective had arrived replayed itself in her head. "You mean you were actually serious about having me stay at the ranch?" She'd assumed that he'd been just talking, throwing the possibility out there so she could roll it over in her mind. What she had decided on was continuing on a path of business as usual instead.

Obviously Whit had other ideas.

"Of course I was serious," he told her. Why would he ask her to stay at his ranch if he wasn't? He didn't understand her reasoning. "I mean, we could stay at my place right here in the city, but it's only got one bedroom, which is a slight drawback," he told her.

The idea of sharing that small of a space with her brought with it a number of problems, not the least of which was that although he'd berated himself for having taken advantage of her and the situation that night in Nevada, he was still very attracted to her.

"And more importantly," he went on, "whoever did that to your car—" he gestured at the vehicle, now being guided onto a flatbed tow truck so it could be brought down to the CSI lab for thorough testing "—knows where I live. It's not exactly a state secret," he reminded her.

"Neither is the location of your family's ranch," Elizabeth pointed out.

"True," he agreed, "but the difference is that there are a lot more people on the ranch. That translates to there being a lot more people besides just me to keep you safe."

She was, by nature, a private person. This had all the earmarks of living in a goldfish bowl, something she did *not* aspire to.

"I don't think I'm really in any danger," Elizabeth protested rather strongly.

She'd had time to think about it and the more she did, the more convinced she was that no one was out to kill her. This was just some kind of perverse warning, although she really didn't have a clue as to what she was being warned about.

Whit was far from convinced. "Well, I don't want to take the chance that you're wrong. Look at it this way. If you're right, you spend some time at a place that a lot of people would kill to be invited to. If I'm right, we're foiling someone's plan to murder you. Not being murdered is always a good thing," he told her wryly. "Try to think of it as a vacation," he urged, then asked her, "When's the last time you had a real vacation?"

Elizabeth frowned. Whit knew the answer to

that as well as she did, she thought, since they frequently interacted with one another at AdAir Corp, not to mention that they went on business trips together. As a matter of fact, not a week went by when they weren't sitting next to one another at some meeting or other. In the five years that she'd worked at AdAir, there hadn't been a single week that had gone by without his having to work with her. She'd never been absent, to his recollection.

"I can't remember," Elizabeth was finally forced to admit.

"Exactly my point," he told her. "That means you're way overdue for one." Holding the passenger side door open for her, he gestured for her to get in. Elizabeth stubbornly stood her ground. "Don't make me have to put you into the car," he said.

Part of her wanted to see if he actually would, but the other part of her *knew* that he wasn't bluffing and she did want to maintain her dignity in this. With a displeased sigh, she got into the passenger side and buckled up. Only then did Whit round his hood and get in on the driver's side.

Buckling up, he lost no time in starting up his sports car. A second later, he took off.

"I take it that your car really does do zero to sixty in ten seconds," she commented.

The second she'd heard the engine all but growling as he gave it gas, she'd grabbed her armrests and held on to them as if they were actual lifelines intended to keep her anchored to earth instead of spinning out into the stratosphere.

She felt as if her stomach had been left behind at the starting line and was now struggling to bring about a reunion. Ordinarily, she would have enjoyed this display of engine power, but not in her present condition.

A few minutes later, Elizabeth realized that Whit was decreasing the car's all but teeth-rattling speed. "Oh, don't do it on my account. I'm kind of curious to find out if my skin is going to fall off after you reach a certain speed."

Whit spared her a smile, but kept the speed at a constant rate now. "Hasn't happened yet."

"Something to look forward to later on," she countered.

He made no comment. Instead, he asked her for her exact address.

Giving it to him, Elizabeth sat back in her seat. Since she had no choice in the matter—and part of her had to admit that she did rather like the idea that Whit was being protective of her—she went into her efficiency mode, mentally going over everything that she was going to need to keep herself productively busy during this sudden so-called vacation she was being forced to take.

She didn't do idle well.

She had everything down pat in her mind by the time Whit brought them to her town house.

Because of the time of day and the fact that most people were at work, Whit had no difficulty finding parking. He eased his sports car into a space directly in front of her town house. Familiar with the way Elizabeth operated, he felt confident that they would be in and out of her home in a very short amount of time.

"You can wait in the car if you like," she told him as she got out. "I won't be long."

He had no intention of remaining outside. Protecting her meant just that to him—*protecting* her. And in order to do that, he had to be *around* her.

"If it's all the same to you," he told her, locking his car, "I'll just come inside."

"Don't trust me?" she asked, thinking that was why he wanted to come with her. Humor curved her mouth. "I promise not to try to escape."

He looked at her as he waited for her to unlock her front door. He noticed the absence of a security system. He was going to have to look into that for her.

"Why would you want to escape? I'm not taking you to Siberia," he quipped.

Elizabeth closed the door behind him. "I just thought you might think—never mind," she said, waving away her explanation. As she replayed it in her head, it sounded too involved and too much like an excuse. She didn't want to get into it.

She wasn't happy about having to go into hiding—because, after all, that's what it really was—but if she had to, then she had to. Whit was the new boss now that his father was dead and as such, she knew that she now had to take her orders from him. This, apparently, was just another order.

"I just thought I could help you pack," he told her. "I'm really quite good at it," he added.

"I'm sure you are," she answered. "But there's no need," she told him crisply. "I'm already packed." She saw the quizzical look he gave her. "I keep a go bag in my closet, packed and ready in case your father wants—wanted," she amended with a frown, "to send me on a trip.

"I am still having the worst time thinking of your father in the past tense," she confessed. Reginald Adair had been so dynamic, so full of life, that thinking of him as deceased—even though she had attended the funeral—was a very difficult adjustment for her.

"Me, too," Whit admitted after a beat.

He paused now to look around the lower level of her town house. Her furnishings appeared to be sparse, as if she didn't spend all that much time here. What there was appeared to be incredibly neat.

It looked more like a model home than a place where someone actually lived.

"What's wrong?" she asked, noting the look on his face.

"Nothing," he answered, then, because she didn't appear satisfied, he amended, "It's just that I kind of expected that you were secretly a messy person—you know, to balance out all that super efficiency that you're always demonstrating at work."

"Sorry to disappoint you," she told him, walking into her bedroom. She raised her voice so he could hear her where he was standing. "I'm just as boring in private as I am on the job."

"I wouldn't call it boring," he told her.

He meant that as a general compliment, but his words managed to arouse a flash of a memory from their one night together at the hotel. *Boring* was the last word he would have ever used to describe Elizabeth. She was anything but that.

"Your organizational abilities are a rare gift, Elizabeth," he told her. "My father would have been lost without you."

"Your father," she said, emerging from her bedroom pulling a small suitcase on wheels behind her, "would have managed just fine without me. He was that kind of a person."

"He might have managed—here, let me," Whit offered, putting his hand right next to hers on the suitcase's handle, "but it definitely wouldn't have been easy," he assured her.

He knew she was being modest, but it almost sounded like a put-down to him. He sincerely doubted that she was actually aware of her true worth in the scheme of things.

But he was.

"I can handle this," Elizabeth told him, her hand still holding on to the suitcase.

"I'm sure you can," Whit agreed, keeping his hand exactly where it was, "but I need to feel chivalrous right now, so I'd consider it a favor if you'd allow me to take your suitcase to my car."

After a second, Elizabeth laughed softly. She pulled back her hand, raising it as if surrendering to his request.

"If you put it that way," she told him, "I really can't say no."

Whit smiled. "I know."

His sports car had only a miniscule trunk, so Whit was forced to place her suitcase in the very limited space available behind his front seat.

Elizabeth got back into the car and buckled up. She waited until Whit started the car again before asking him the question that had been weighing rather heavily on her mind.

"Who else is going to be there at the ranch?"

"Landry and Carson. Landry still lives there, but my brother is staying at the ranch only until he can find a place of his own," Whit explained. "For the last few years, he's been in the Marines, so adjusting to civilian life is a little tricky for him after having been deployed to the Middle East. He wants to make the adjustment before he decides where he's going to live and more or less what he wants to do with the rest of his life."

Elizabeth could only imagine how his brother had to feel. Here he was, newly discharged from the Marines, only to come home and have his father murdered. Violence could slip into the most seemingly tranquil areas of people's lives, she thought. The AdAir Corp building was the last place she would have expected a murder to take place.

"Is that everyone?" she wanted to know. She had a feeling that it wasn't.

"Well, there's the cook and the housekeeper…" Whit paused before added, "And there's my mother." Out of the corner of his eye, he saw Elizabeth visibly stiffen. He was quick to try to assuage her reaction. "Mother lives in her own quarters at the ranch. They're totally separate from the rest of the house," he assured her. "She wanted it that way. When Landry was away at school and Carson was in the Marines, at times, besides the servants, there were just my parents in that big house and they could go for days without their paths crossing if they were having one of their epic disagreements."

Listening, Elizabeth found that profoundly

sad. Why bother staying married if they wanted to spend all their time apart?

But she kept her thoughts on the matter to herself. It wasn't any of her business and she was certain that Whit wouldn't have welcomed any questions or comments on his parents' rather isolated lifestyle. She had no doubt that it probably bothered him a great deal when he thought about it.

Still, despite her separate quarters, the fact that Whit's mother lived on the ranch presented her with an immediate dilemma. The ranch might have belonged to the family, but Elizabeth was certain that Patsy Adair considered the house to be hers.

Staying there for any amount of time—even a short amount of time—placed her in a very awkward position, Elizabeth thought.

"Your mother's definitely *not* going to be happy about my staying at the ranch—unless you plan to stash me in some of the closets, slipping my meals under the door," she added wryly, coming up with the only scenario that she felt would appeal somewhat to Mrs. Adair.

"No closet," Whit assured her with a laugh. "And my mother will be just fine with your staying at the ranch. First of all, the place is huge and you could both go for days without accidentally running into one another—"

"I'd really rather not stay there under those

kinds of circumstances," she told Whit, bracing herself for an argument.

She didn't believe in being difficult, but the circumstances as they were outlined were not acceptable to her. She didn't do well in that sort of a scenario—one in which she was regarded with disdain. The reason for that disdain was transparent. Patsy Adair felt that her husband and his executive assistant had been lovers. And Elizabeth knew that the more she might try to deny the very thought of that kind of a relationship between her and the now deceased president of AdAir Corp, the guiltier she would undoubtedly look.

So her best recourse was silence—as frustrating as that might be.

"Luckily for you, you won't have to," Whit told her. "Because as it happens, my mother loves company above all else." The *right kind* of company, he added silently. In his mother's case, that meant celebrities and captains of industry, as well as a few high-ranking political officials. But he saw no point in dwelling on that right now. "She might have had a few sharp words to say at the reading of the will, but don't forget, she was still trying to deal with all these unexpected twists and turns— the biggest of which was my father's murder."

Despite her dramatics, Patsy Adair did not strike Elizabeth as a genuinely grieving widow, only a woman playacting the part of a supposedly grieving widow, she thought.

She didn't find the woman all that convincing.

"I understand all that," Elizabeth told him quietly. "But to be very blunt about it—" something she was admittedly less than happy to be, especially in this case "—I don't think your mother really likes me. Having me staying *indefinitely*—" she emphasized the word "—at her house—"

"The *family* house," he corrected.

"You and your siblings might think of it that way," Elizabeth granted, "but I'm willing to bet that your mother views the ranch as her own personal domain. Especially now that your father is gone."

He couldn't bring himself to argue the point with Elizabeth. With everything as charged as it was right now, he sincerely doubted that he could change her mind at the moment.

In truth, he had never regarded the woman who was his mother as the warm, motherly type, not even when he'd been a little boy.

For the most part, Patsy Adair was the beautiful stranger who made sporadic guest appearances in his life and the lives of his brother and sister. They had never had a warm, loving relationship—or any sort of real relationship to speak of—with the woman. Her DNA ran through his blood, but she was a mother in name only and only when it suited her to be, such as when a photo op presented itself.

But be that as it may, that didn't change the fact that the house belonged to all of them according to the terms of the will, which meant, bottom line, that he could bring anyone he wanted to the ranch.

And he wanted to bring Elizabeth.

That was all there was to it. End of argument, he thought.

Out loud he told Elizabeth, "It'll be all right," and left it at that, because they both knew that he had always been as good as his word.

But there was always a first time for everything, Elizabeth couldn't help thinking. And this time around just might be that time.

Chapter 9

When he and Elizabeth arrived at Adair Acres a little while later, Whit drove his car up the long driveway right to the front door of the twelve-thousand-square-foot Spanish-style house.

Getting out on his side, he noticed that Elizabeth remained where she was, making no effort to get out. He thought it was rather odd, but decided that perhaps she was waiting for him to open her door. It struck him as being completely out of character for the Elizabeth he knew, but he played along and came around to her side to hold the door open for her.

Elizabeth still didn't move. Instead, she continued sitting in her seat, buckled up and looking at the sprawling hacienda.

Rather than question her about her behavior, Whit decided to inject a little humor into the situation. It was a weapon that he seldom used but felt she might respond to.

"I could have your meals brought out here if you like, but I don't think you're going to enjoy sleeping in the car, especially since I'd be forced to sleep in it, too. Not much space for both of us to spend a prolonged amount of time in."

Elizabeth looked at him, one eyebrow raised in a silent request for an explanation. "Why would you have to stay in the car with me?"

"I said I'd look out for you, and I can't do that from the house if you're out here. I'd have to stay out here, too," Whit concluded. He pretended to regard the seat behind the steering wheel. "Really looks pretty uncomfortable from where I'm standing."

He heard her sigh. The next moment, Elizabeth was shifting to one side and climbing out of the front passenger seat.

Her expression looked resigned as well as grim. Was it because she wasn't in control of things or was there another reason for her less-than-thrilled look, he couldn't help wondering.

"Relax," he urged. "You're acting as if you're walking into the dentist's office."

"No, I'm not," she replied matter-of-factly. "My dentist likes me."

He didn't get a chance to comment on her reply or to assure her that everyone here at the ranch liked her as well, because just then the front door flew open and Landry came hurrying out.

Her blue eyes bright with curiosity, Landry didn't bother with acknowledgments but went straight to the question she'd been dying to ask for the past couple of hours.

"Is it true?" she asked eagerly, looking from her brother to the woman he'd brought with him.

"Say hello to the nice houseguest, Landry," Whit prompted his sister, taking Elizabeth's suitcase from the backseat. It took a little angling before he could finally get it out.

Rather than do as her brother said, Landry threw her arms around Elizabeth and hugged the other woman hard. "You're all right!" she cried, delighted to verify that part of the information for herself.

Elizabeth automatically stiffened in response to the enthusiastic hug. With effort, she forced herself to do as Whit had counseled and relaxed. Displays of affection—both giving them and being on the receiving end—had always been difficult for her because it meant allowing her guard to go down, and that led to all sorts of complications she didn't want to entertain. The only one she had ever let her guard down with was Whit—and look where that had gotten her: rebuffed, as well as pregnant.

But the young woman who had thrown her arms around her was obviously sweet and genuine. After a beat, Elizabeth allowed herself to hug Landry back.

Three years younger than her late father's executive assistant, Landry was also three inches taller than Elizabeth, not to mention that she came on like gangbusters.

Whit shook his head. His little sister, he knew, could be rather overwhelming at times and she had no idea that she was.

"Let her breathe, Landry. You've got Elizabeth almost in a death grip and you're damn near cutting off her air supply."

Whit's words suddenly penetrated her consciousness and Landry released her brother's unexpected houseguest. "Oh, I'm sorry. So sorry," she repeated, dropping her hands to her sides as she stepped back, creating a little space between herself and Elizabeth. "I didn't mean to hurt you."

Elizabeth smiled at the other young woman. Landry made her think of a young colt, all legs and skittish enthusiasm, trying to run off in three directions at once. "You didn't," she told the youngest of Reginald's offspring.

"No," Whit deadpanned, "you always turn that shade of blue."

Landry shot her brother an exasperated look.
The next moment, looking away, she forgot all
about the teasing remark. "Are you really staying here with us?" Landry sounded absolutely
delighted at the prospect. The next moment, she
confirmed it. "That's wonderful!"

The younger woman went to hug Elizabeth
again, then, remembering her brother's admon-
ishment, she raised her hands in mock surrender.
Instead, she grabbed the older woman's hand in
both of hers and gave it a warm, heartfelt squeeze.
"Having you here is going to be great!" she cried.
"I was really beginning to feel outnumbered here,
what with Whit and Carson practically forming a
good ol' boys' club and ganging up on me." Landry
all but beamed at the other woman. "It'll be nice
to have you around to round out the odds a little."

Elizabeth looked at her a little uncertainly.
Maybe there was some hope to be gleaned here.
"Isn't your mother around?"

The slight frown on the younger woman's lips
told Elizabeth that Landry didn't consider her
mother an ally in any manner.

"Only when she wants to be and she's not on
any side except her own," Landry confided. Just
as she was leading Elizabeth toward the staircase,
she stopped abruptly and turned around to face
her. "I almost forgot—is it true?" she asked, get-

ting back to the initial question she'd posed when she first saw Elizabeth.

That was the phrase she'd greeted them with, Whit thought. Her question wasn't any clearer to him now than it was then. "Is *what* true?"

Rather than answer Whit, his sister looked at Elizabeth. "Did someone try to kill you?"

"No." And she was going to cling to that, Elizabeth thought. To think anything else would begin to paralyze her and then she wouldn't be able to get things accomplished. She *needed* to get things done. This wasn't the time for self-indulgence. "They slashed my tires," Elizabeth corrected.

"Isn't that the same thing?" Landry asked, puzzled. She looked from their houseguest to her older brother.

"Only if she was driving on them when they were slashed," Whit told her matter-of-factly. It wasn't something he was prepared to dwell on. He noted the thoughtful look on his sister's face. "Don't strain your brain, Lan. It's not exactly a recommended way to kill someone."

"Who are we killing?" Carson asked, drawn by the sound of their voices and walking into the expansive front room.

"Nobody," Whit said firmly.

At the same time, Landry volunteered, "Elizabeth," in response to the former marine's question.

Carson's eyes shifted to the newcomer and nodded a greeting. Amusement curved the corners of his sensual mouth. "Any particular reason we're killing Elizabeth?" he asked, tongue-in-cheek.

"*We're* not killing Elizabeth." Landry spoke up before Whit did. "But someone else tried to. She had the tires on her car slashed."

Carson's easy smile faded and he looked both concerned and very serious as he asked, "Who did it?"

"That's what we're still trying to find out," Whit told him.

Carson's bright blue eyes—so like his brother's—shifted to look at Elizabeth. "Are you all right?" he asked her.

It wasn't in her to cause concern or play the part of a defenseless victim. She was and always had been in charge of her own life and willing and able to take care of herself. Now was no different.

"I'm fine," she automatically assured Carson, even though she secretly had to admit that her nerves felt shot. Though she wouldn't admit it out loud, staying here with Whit's family around her did go a long way to making her feel better about the situation.

"What are the police doing about it?" Carson asked Whit. Knowing his brother—they hadn't been close for a while now, but some things were just a given—he was fairly certain that Whit had called in the police the second the slashed tires were discovered.

"What they always do," Whit said with a note of impatient disgust in his voice. "They took notes and then disappeared into the woodwork."

"Where did this happen?" Carson wanted to know, turning to Elizabeth.

"In Miller's parking lot," Whit answered, referring to the family lawyer.

Carson looked confused. "But we were just there," he protested.

"I know," Whit confirmed. "Obviously whoever did it felt pretty confident they wouldn't be noticed until it was too late."

Carson frowned. There was more than a little truth in that. "In the right setting and with enough distraction, the Hulk wouldn't be noticed. So what are *we* doing about it?" he asked Whit.

"Not much we can do right now." And he made no secret of the fact that it bothered the hell out of him. "Elizabeth's going to stay here at the house for a few days, until we hopefully get some answers," Whit told his brother and sister.

He studied both of them to see if any objections registered on either of their faces. Neither looked upset or even mildly disturbed at the prospect of having the woman as a houseguest.

"If you don't mind," Elizabeth felt bound to add, looking from Landry to Carson.

She couldn't shake the feeling that she was imposing by staying here, despite the size of the house. She hadn't taken it all in yet, but she was quite certain that she could have easily fit at least five models of her town house into the massive hacienda.

"The more the merrier," Carson assured her.

"It'll be fun," was Landry's response, her eyes all but gleaming brightly.

"See, I told you nobody would object," Whit reminded her.

"Yet," Elizabeth tagged on, looking at him pointedly. He knew exactly what she was talking about—and whom—Elizabeth thought.

"You mean Mother?" Carson asked. Reading between the lines wasn't exactly a challenge in this case. "Don't worry about her," he told Elizabeth with a dismissive wave of his hand. "She hardly ever comes out of her lair when it's just us. Apparently she doesn't consider us to be in her league or entertaining enough for her to waste time with," he said, adding, "There has to be someone here she feels is worth the effort before she comes out to spend some time with the rest of us."

Did they all feel that way? Elizabeth wondered. She had no family of her own, no siblings to turn to or share things with. She'd been on her own from a very young age, and while that had helped to make her independent and self-sufficient, it had also made her emotionally vacant. She often thought that if she'd had a family, things would have been different—and more than likely better.

But listening to Carson as well as Whit made her think that perhaps she'd taken too much for granted when it came to familial support.

Well, either way there was nothing she could do about that, she told herself. No matter how much time she spent thinking about it, it wasn't going to give her a family of her own.

She was destined to go on alone and, for the most part, she had resigned herself to that.

"Don't pay attention to Carson," Landry told her with a laugh, taking her off to one side for a moment. "He's been away for a while and it's made him forget how things are around here."

Carson took the opportunity to corner his brother for a moment. "Listen, Whit, I wanted to talk to you about that little bombshell that Miller dropped on us today," he began.

Whit wanted to take Elizabeth upstairs to show her to her room—there were two set aside specifically for guests—but since Landry had button-holed her for a minute, he decided to hear Carson out. He was curious to see if Carson was having the same kind of thoughts on the matter as he was.

"You mean that little detail about there being another son nobody ever knew anything about?" There was an edge of sarcasm in Whit's voice.

"Yeah, that," Carson said cryptically. "You know, since I've come back I'm kind of at loose ends here, so I thought maybe I'd use my time to see if I can track down this so-called missing older brother Dad forgot to tell us about instead of just hiring some stranger to do it for us."

Whit nodded. "I was beginning to think the same thing," he admitted, rescinding his original thought about hiring a private detective. "You know, now that I think about it, I can see Dad keeping something like this from us," Whit said.

While he assumed that his father had cared about his family in some fashion, the man had never demonstrated any notable affection or made any real effort to be a substantial part of their lives.

"He was never much for sharing or talking," Whit added.

Landry looked up, catching the last part of her brother's sentence.

"To *you*," Landry emphasized. "Dad was never close to either one of *you*." She wasn't bragging. As far as she was concerned, this was just the regrettable way things had been. "But I thought he and I were close. I guess I was wrong," she concluded sadly. The sparkle temporarily left her eyes as she said, "I guess nobody ever knows anyone as well as they think they do."

"Ah, but an air of mystery spices things up a bit, don't you think?"

All four people in the room turned toward the source of the somewhat sarcastic comment. Caught up in their conversation, no one had heard Patsy Adair approaching until the shapely platinum blonde was right there in their midst.

Always looking as if she was dressed to go out on the town, the smirk on Patsy's lips deepened as her eyes swept critically over the gathering of young people she had walked in on.

Her attention shifted to the one nonfamily member in the room. Patsy's eyes narrowed just a touch even though her mouth remained curved in a smile that appeared pasted on at best.

"Elizabeth, dear. You do seem to turn up in the most unlikely places. Have you brought something for AdAir Corp's acting president to consider?" she asked, briefly touching Whit's arm as if to indicate that she was referring to him as she mentioned the position so recently vacated by her late husband.

Her tone continued to be deceptively light and the smile remained on her lips. But the latter didn't reach her eyes and in effect was nearly as shallow as her tone.

It was very evident that although she was smiling, Patsy was *not* welcoming the younger woman to her home with open arms.

If anything, the exact opposite was true.

"Or have you decided to drop by for dinner?"

She turned toward Whit. "Did you neglect to tell me someone was coming to dinner, dear? Or did I just not hear you when you mentioned it?"

What game was she playing now, Whit wondered, exasperated. It took effort to keep his voice civil. "Elizabeth will be staying here for a few days," Whit told her. "And I didn't know you cared enough about these sorts of things to want to be notified."

"Why, dear, I care about everything that goes on here at Adair Acres," Patsy told her oldest son, patting his cheek lightly.

The condescending movement was lost on no one in the room.

Elizabeth's eyes locked with Whit's, silently telling him *I told you.*

She struggled with the strong desire to leave the house. Only the fact that she didn't want Patsy to feel as if she had chased her away kept Elizabeth standing where she was.

"Is there a specific reason she's staying here?" Patsy asked, looking at her older son for an answer while deliberately treating Elizabeth as if she were an inanimate object. "Or did she just arbitrarily decide to slip into your bed because she doesn't like to sleep alone and your father's bed isn't an option for her any longer?"

Whit slanted a quick look in Elizabeth's direction, deep regret in his eyes. His apology went without saying. He didn't want her to endure being belittled by his mother.

"Mother," Whit said sharply, conveying both his displeasure and issuing a warning wrapped around the single tersely voiced word.

Patsy raised a bejeweled hand in the universal surrender sign. "I'll behave, dear. No need to get all hot under the collar. I was just trying to determine what was prompting Lizzy's visit."

"Elizabeth. Her name is Elizabeth," Whit told his mother coldly.

"Of course it is, and I know that," she said, humoring her firstborn. "But a nickname is so much friendlier, don't you think?" his mother asked with what might have looked like an innocent expression on anyone else's face. On Patsy's face, it appeared strangely malevolent. Turning to give Elizabeth her full attention, Patsy asked, "Will you be dining with us, *Elizabeth*?"

"I think the question here is are *you* going to be dining with *us*?" Whit countered. "Since you hardly ever do."

He couldn't really remember the last time they'd sat at the dining room table as a family. Now, of course, with his father's death, that was never going to happen.

"Why, darling, it would be rude not to," Patsy said loftily. "I wouldn't miss it for the world." She turned her smile up another few watts as she flashed it at Elizabeth. "I'll see you at dinner, dear. I'll be counting the minutes."

And with that, the woman withdrew from the room, leaving the other four occupants speechless— just as she had clearly intended to do.

Chapter 10

Elizabeth was the first one to speak up after Reginald Adair's widow left the front room. Looking at Whit, she repeated what she had already made known to him previously.

"This was a bad idea, my staying here." She looked at the suitcase Whit had parked by the sofa. "I should go."

"No, it's not a bad idea," Landry insisted before Elizabeth could claim her suitcase and head for the door. "You *should* stay here with us so you can stay safe. Don't let Mother chase you away. She doesn't really mean half the things she says—it's just her way. I know that deep down she really likes you."

Elizabeth didn't believe it for a moment, but it was obvious that Landry did, and since the younger woman was being so sweet to her, she cut her some slack.

"Well, then it has to be really deep, deep down," Elizabeth told her, "because I doubt if your mother is aware of it."

"It doesn't matter if she is or not," Whit told her with finality. "You're here because you need a bodyguard watching over you and that is exactly what I intend to be. Your bodyguard."

"Don't you already have enough job titles on your résumé?" Elizabeth pointed out. "You don't have time to babysit me."

His eyes met hers. She didn't, he noted, look away or back down. He had to admit that he admired someone who couldn't be cowed into giving up. He liked her style, but then, he already knew that. The hard part was keeping that from showing.

"I'm acting president of AdAir Corp," Whit reminded her. "What that means is that I have time for anything I say I have time for."

He made it clear that he left no room to contest his position.

"I guess I can't argue with you," Elizabeth said, surrendering—for now.

"Oh, you can argue," Whit told her. "You just won't win. Now let me show you to your room."

"And then I get dibs on her," Landry said,

speaking up as her brother and Elizabeth turned toward the winding staircase. "The poor woman needs a break from being browbeaten by you," she informed Whit. She flashed a smile at Elizabeth and promised, "It'll be fun."

Elizabeth forced a quick, small smile onto her lips. Fun had never been high on her priority list. Reaching goals, getting projects accomplished— those always took precedence over wasting time kicking back and essentially being nonproductive.

Maybe that was the problem, Elizabeth thought. Maybe she'd been missing out. Maybe, as she'd heard said over and over again, it wasn't the destination so much as the journey that was really important.

Maybe she needed to pay a little more attention to that, to the journey, she told herself.

However, she sincerely had her doubts if she could, because it would take concentrated effort to change at this point and as far as she was concerned, she had finally gotten her act together, and made peace with who she was.

Well, change is coming, Lizzy, whether you like it or not, a little voice inside her reminded her. *That little passenger you're carrying around will see to that.*

She'd forgotten about that for a moment.

With effort Elizabeth pushed the thought away for now.

"That would be nice," she told Landry just before she followed Whit and her suitcase up the stairs.

Whit brought her to a room halfway down the hallway on the second floor.

"This is it," he told her, opening the door. He gestured inside the room.

Elizabeth stood in the doorway, momentarily frozen in place, feeling a little like Dorothy Gale lifted out of Kansas and getting her very first view of Oz.

"This is your *guest* room?" she asked, disbelief and wonder echoing in her voice.

"Yes." Whit couldn't tell by her tone of voice exactly what she was thinking. Some people, he knew, were turned off by any visible signs of affluence, and Adair Acres wallowed in it. His mother had had a hand in elaborately decorating every square inch of the extensive hacienda.

"Who was your last guest?" Elizabeth asked in sheer wonder. "The queen of England?"

Glancing at her, Whit saw the awe in her eyes. "I take it that means you like what you see," he said with a laugh.

"Like it?" Elizabeth echoed. "If this room was portable, I'd steal it." Moving to the center of the bedroom, she looked around very slowly until she had turned a full 360 degrees. "Someone could certainly have one hell of a massive party in here."

Whit continued observing her, studying her every move, finding that he was having more and more trouble keeping a viable distance between the two of them. That was especially problematic since he kept finding little things about her that were successfully reeling him in, appealing to his more chivalrous side as well as to the male within him. The latter part had wound up being so aroused by her that one night they spent together in Nevada.

He honestly would have given anything for that night not to have taken place—but even so, at the same time all he could think about was having her just one more time. It wasn't that he felt that he'd be satisfied with that one more time—it would just mean that he'd have that much more of a memory in his brain to activate.

Whit was well aware of the fact that he was being greedy.

He knew, too, that one more taste of forbidden fruit—they were, after all, associates—would not begin to satiate his appetite for her, but it would at least give him that much more to savor.

And he would *have* to be satisfied with that, he told himself firmly.

To his dismay, Whit found himself being aroused just by looking at her. "It doesn't have to be massive to be a party," he told her quietly.

"I know," she agreed just as quietly, her throat suddenly becoming as dry as a desert as she turned to look at Whit. She could feel her adrenaline kicking in, could feel her heart doing a quick two-step. She had to remind herself to breathe. "Sometimes the best parties have only two participants."

She realized that somehow, without orchestrating it, they had both moved so they were standing mere inches apart from one another. So close that she could feel his breath skimming along her face.

Goose bumps of anticipation were forming all up and down her arms and even her own breath had become short—when she breathed at all.

"You're right," he replied, his eyes ever so lightly brushing along the outline of her lips before they returned to her eyes. "All this talk of parties has put me in a party mood."

His eyes were holding hers captive and she just couldn't make herself look away, afraid that if she did, all of this—the moment, the promise, the man—would just fade away and vanish, as if she had imagined all of it.

Except that she hadn't.

"You, too?" Elizabeth asked in a barely audible whisper.

"Me, too," he whispered back, his voice deep and husky.

The momentary silence that followed was all but deafening. Whit framed her face with his hands. The next second, he kissed her. Kissed her like a man who had been aching to kiss her for a long, long time.

Kissed her like a man who knew about the precious, wonderfully sweet taste of her lips that lay waiting for him.

Half an eternity later, he dropped his hands from her face and wrapped his arms around her instead. He held her to him as he kissed her deeply and with feeling.

Her head was spinning and her heart was racing from the kiss when she heard him promise, "I won't let anything happen to you. I swear," he added after a beat, as if sealing his promise.

Had he done that to convince her that he was serious? "You don't have to add that," she told Whit. "I believe you."

Could he feel it, she wondered. Could he feel that he had her heart racing so fast she could hardly catch her breath? He was stealing it away from her just as he had stolen her heart.

This was *not* supposed to be happening, she silently insisted. And yet it was.

She couldn't contain the burst of sunshine exploding within her.

"I'm sorry about my mother," he told her. He'd drawn back his lips from hers, but he was still holding her in his arms.

She supposed, in an offbeat sort of way, she could understand what Patsy Adair was trying to do. "She's only trying to keep her family safe, same as you," Elizabeth told him.

Elizabeth, he decided, was an incredibly kind, forgiving person.

"She's only trying to keep herself safe," he contradicted. "Listen, if you'd rather go out somewhere for dinner instead of possibly having to endure her snide remarks—"

For all he knew, his mother might just change her mind and not join them for dinner. He never knew until the last moment what his mother was up to. Sometimes not even then.

She couldn't ask him to go out to dinner. "You've already put yourself out for me far more than you needed to. I'll be fine eating right here in your dining room." Her mouth quirked in a philosophical smile. "Your mother's just sharpening her tongue on me. I've endured worse," she confided.

"From who?" he wanted to know, fairly confident that she was just saying that so he wouldn't feel bad about the way his mother was behaving.

For a moment, Elizabeth debated saying anything at all about the subject. This wasn't exactly something she liked to share, or even something she *did* share. It was a page out of her life that she had done her best to bury, placing it in a very dark corner of her mind and shutting the door.

But he was putting himself out for her when he didn't have to. She owed him.

"My mother," Elizabeth finally said, thinking that sharing this bit of information with a man who had, perhaps, gone through the same exact sort of thing in his adolescence might help her deal with the way she felt—or couldn't feel, as the case might be.

There was sympathy in his strikingly blue eyes. "What did she do?" he asked.

"Things I'd rather not talk about," Elizabeth answered, adding, "Not all women should have children. Some are just not equipped with enough patience to put up with the rigors of raising a child."

Whit read between the lines. "Did she hurt you?" he asked.

She saw the anger in his eyes. For a moment, that was *all* she saw.

She'd never had a white knight before. She'd never even had a knight of *any* kind before, she thought in amusement. This was a whole new sensation and it required some adjustment on her part. The largest adjustment had to do with trust. As a rule, she didn't trust—not when it came to personal things. But she owed it to Whit to try her best.

"There are scars," she answered vaguely. And there were, both on her body and more importantly, on her soul. Those were the ones that wouldn't heal. "But they're all in the past. There's no point in revisiting any of them now."

Her shrug was vaguely dismissive of the power those scars had over her.

"They've made me stronger," she told him. "In a weird way, my mother taking her frustrations out on me helped make me the person I am today. I'm able to withstand almost anything."

She needed to change the subject. Revisiting a section of her childhood stirred up feelings she'd thought to be dead long ago. Obviously, they either hadn't died or they just refused to stay dead.

Either way, she needed to rebury them, which in turn meant she had to think of something else and put as much distance between herself and her painful past as she could.

"I think this house should come with maps handed out at the front door." And then she laughed softly. "This *room* should come with a map. I think I've seen pictures of palaces that were smaller than this place," Elizabeth confessed. "What do you *do* with all this room?" she wanted to know.

"Mainly collect dust," he told her, then whimsically added, "And stash away guests."

"In other words, don't open any closets unless otherwise instructed?"

He grinned. "You're catching on."

His grin, Elizabeth noted, was disarming. She

needed to get back to where the other members of his family were. She just couldn't trust the reactions she was having to Whit.

And they were getting stronger…

The quick rap on the partially open door interrupted anything further that Elizabeth might have said to Whit.

Thank God, she thought. The cavalry had arrived.

There was no need to ask who was knocking because the next moment, Landry popped into the room. "So, do you like it?" she asked Whit's houseguest, indicating the room.

"It's magnificent," Elizabeth told her honestly.

Landry looked around, as if seeing the room for the first time through the eyes of a stranger— a wealthy stranger, since she had no other frame of reference.

"It's a little small," Landry said, "but it has a cozy appeal."

"Cozy?" Elizabeth echoed in somewhat amused disbelief. "In comparison to this, the Grand Canyon is cozy." This, she couldn't help thinking, gave new meaning to the phrase *living large*.

"The Grand Canyon, huh?" Landry echoed, seriously turning the comparison over in her mind. "I never thought of it that way," she confessed.

The next second, she was back on track of her original mission: to extract her late father's executive assistant from her workaholic brother's clutches. Knowing Whit, he would probably get Elizabeth to work on some contract with him that was due before the week was out. For the past few years, that was all her older brother ever did: work.

"Anyway, you've monopolized Elizabeth long enough, big brother," Landry declared, placing herself between him and Elizabeth. "It's my turn now to spend some time with her."

"Okay." A flicker of concern entered his brilliant blue eyes. It wasn't that he didn't want Landry spending time with Elizabeth—it was just that he had always thought of her as being somewhat young for her age. Maybe it was because she was the baby of the family, but whatever the reason, he worried about his sister's ability to be aware of her surroundings. "But if something seems off to you, I want you to come find me."

"What if it's you that seems off to me?" Landry asked, struggling to keep a straight face.

He hardly heard her. Whit didn't believe in taking unnecessary chances. "Maybe I should stick around," he decided.

"Maybe you shouldn't," Landry countered. "Elizabeth and I want to spend a little quality girl time together." She spared the smaller woman a nod, as if they had already conferred about this. "And in case you haven't made the connection, girl time requires girls. *Strictly* girls. So unless there's something you haven't been telling me, that disqualifies you from hanging around. Now shoo," Landry ordered, fanning Whit away with her hands as if she was fending off some undesirable animal that was crossing her path.

He supposed that maybe he worried too much. After all, Landry and Elizabeth were going to be not just on the grounds, but inside the house. If they weren't safe here, then they wouldn't be safe anywhere.

"I'll see you later," he told Elizabeth, then turned his attention one last time to his sister. "Remember, call me if you think anything's wrong or out of sync."

Landry elaborately crossed her heart as if she were swearing a sacred oath.

Rolling his eyes heavenward, Whit murmured something unintelligible under his breath and withdrew.

"Honestly," Landry said, closing the door behind her departing brother, "I thought we'd never get rid of him. I mean, I love Whit and all, I really do, but he worries too much and he's too strait-laced. There are times when I think he just kind of sucks all the air up in the room."

"He means well." Elizabeth was quick to come to Whit's defense. Her pulse had yet to settle down to normal after that kiss in the guest room. Granted, he did come on strong, but his father *had* been murdered and her tires *had* been slashed while she was parked in Adair's lawyer's parking lot. Offhand, she would have said that Whit had a good reason for being as overprotective as he was.

"Yes, I know he means well," Landry agreed. "But he definitely needs work," she insisted. "Don't get me wrong, I'm crazy about him, I really am, but I also know that he's got flaws."

That came as no surprise, Elizabeth thought. "Most people do."

"Yes, but most people aren't part of my family. Whit is. Mind you, I can't blame him for being so uptight and removed at the same time. That's his way of coping with his childhood—*our* childhood," Landry amended. "None of us exactly have sterling examples of what love and marriage—a *good* marriage—are supposed to be like. Our boilerplate for marriage involved shouting, breaking glass and slamming doors—and that was just the warm-up." She shook her head sadly. "My parents should never have gotten married."

"But if they hadn't, then none of you would have ever been born," Elizabeth pointed out with a soft smile. There was something about the younger woman that spoke to her. She'd felt a bond forming between them the first time she'd laid eyes on Landry. The girl belonged to a cluster of people who were just instantly likable. "And the world would have missed out on that."

Landry hooked her arm through hers. "*Knew* I liked you for a reason," she declared, grinning broadly. "C'mon, let's go to my room. It's got way more stuff than this room."

And obviously, Elizabeth thought, Landry set a high premium on stuff. The younger woman's enthusiasm amused her. Elizabeth saw no reason not to go along and indulge her.

After showing her her room, Landry decided that a proper tour of the grounds might be in order. The first place she brought her to was the barn.

"That's right, you have horses, don't you?" Elizabeth recalled as she followed behind Whit's sister.

"No, we don't have horses," Landry replied. "We have magnificent examples of horseflesh. Each is a champion in his or her own right."

As if to prove her point, Landry brought her over to their prize stallion.

Elizabeth was attracted to the stallion almost instantly. "He's beautiful," she whispered, crossing to the horse.

"Boy horses don't like being called beautiful," Landry informed her, then winked. "But he is, isn't he?" she agreed like a fellow conspirator. "Thunder, this is Elizabeth. Elizabeth, meet Thunder." The horse rubbed his muzzle against her, as if asking to be petted. "Hey, he seems to like you. A lot. I think I'm jealous," Landry teased. "Thunder likes you better than he likes me. And

I've even got sugar cubes in my pocket." She dug into her pocket. "Here," she said, handing Elizabeth one. "Put it in the center of your palm and offer it to him."

Elizabeth did as she was told and laughed softly as Thunder gently separated the cube from her hand.

"Ah, if only two-legged men were as easy to control and have eating out of your hand," Landry said with a wistful sigh.

"I'll settle for this," Elizabeth replied, stroking Thunder's muzzle. At least a horse couldn't break your heart, she thought.

Chapter 11

She made a habit of having the ringer on her cell phone turned off, setting her cell phone to vibrate instead. She didn't want to disturb anyone with her phone, but she didn't want to miss a call either. There was the off chance that it might be the police calling, or one of Adair's associates or friends. Then, of course, it could always be Whit, needing her help with something.

Elizabeth made it a point never to miss any of the calls. Which was why she found herself on the receiving end of calls coming from phone numbers that were intentionally blocked. Whenever she picked up one of those, she would hear someone quickly hanging up on the other end. It didn't matter if she answered on the first ring or the tenth. Whoever was calling always hung up as soon as she said hello. Why? Was it a cruel game meant to drive her crazy? Or what?

Elizabeth kept telling herself that it was all in her head. That it was just a product of her overactive imagination, something she hadn't realized that she possessed until all this murder-and-slashed-tires business had started.

But these calls, as well as other things, were getting to her, making her feel steadily more uneasy. It made Elizabeth wonder if she could really trust her own judgment.

She knew that Whit had noticed that she was ill at ease. He thought it was because his mother seemed to be around more than she usually was, and Elizabeth supposed that in part, Patsy Adair was the problem. She didn't like being where she wasn't wanted and whatever Landry maintained to the contrary, Elizabeth was certain that Whit's mother did *not* like her or want her staying there at the ranch.

As a matter of fact, whenever Patsy smiled at her, it made her blood run cold, as if she had just stared into the face of death. A very attractive death—because Patsy *was* that—but nonetheless, a very final death.

"You're acting jumpier," Whit commented after

noting the subtle shift in her behavior during the week that she had been here at the ranch.

"Maybe it's because I have nothing to do but think," Elizabeth replied, grasping at the first excuse she could come up with. She didn't want him to think she was ungrateful to him, nor did she want him to think she was a whiner. But the truth of it was she was going stir-crazy. "If I had something concrete to do, if I had less time on my hands to do nothing but think and breathe, I wouldn't have time to be jumpy."

She was making sense, Whit thought. In her position, he'd be exactly the same way. "I guess this vacation isn't exactly turning out to be one, is it?"

Elizabeth hesitated, then shook her head. "No— not that I don't appreciate what you're trying to do," she was quick to add. The last thing she wanted to do was offend him.

He wasn't looking for her appreciation. "What I am trying to do, Elizabeth, is to keep you alive."

They were standing in the front room, near the large bay window that had a spectacular view of the front of the family acreage. Elizabeth sighed and looked off to the horizon, watching a formation of birds making their way across the sky.

"I know that and I *am* grateful," she told him. "I'm sorry, I didn't mean to complain. I'm afraid you just caught me off guard."

There was just a hint of a smile teasing the cor-

ners of his mouth. "So you had no prepared statement ready for me?"

Elizabeth started to protest, then realized it
would be better all around if she just went along
with what he was assuming.

"You got me," she told him, raising her hands
slightly like a cornered suspect who had been
found guilty.

He thought a moment, intent on rectifying her
restless feeling. And then he thought he had come
up with an answer. "We're going to be looking into
starting a new advertising campaign to launch the
new cell phones that'll be available with our service this summer. Why don't I have the information sent from the office to your personal laptop
tomorrow? You can start work on that. Would that
make you feel better?" he asked.

Better? She could have thrown her arms around
him and kissed him—again—but that would only
start another line of trouble.

"Infinitely!" she cried eagerly.

Whit inclined his head, as if making it happen
right there on the spot.

"Consider it done. I'll just make a few calls,"
he told her. "And Elizabeth," he began just before
he began to walk away.

She still hadn't moved and she looked at him
now, wondering if he was going to say he'd
changed his mind. "Yes?"

"It's going to be okay," he said, making a silent promise to her at the same time.

"Absolutely," Elizabeth replied with whole-hearted enthusiasm.

Whit paused in the far doorway for a moment, one eyebrow raised a little higher than the other as he scrutinized her. She hadn't exactly convinced him. "You're just humoring me, aren't you?"

The smile lit up her eyes first. "Absolutely," she repeated.

"Why wait? I'll get on having that information forwarded right away," he told her as he left the room.

That was just what she needed, Elizabeth thought as she went upstairs to the opulent suite that was her bedroom. She needed work. Something to get her mind off both this supposed threat against her—a threat that was causing her to imagine accidents waiting to happen around every corner, hiding in every shadow—and the accident that had *already* happened. Namely the baby she was carrying—and concealing.

Entering her temporary quarters, Elizabeth stopped to look herself over in the floor-to-ceiling mirror near one of the closets in the room. Specifically, she was looking intently and critically at her profile—her *lower* profile—in the mirror.

She was flat as a board.

Counting forward from that fateful night, she

knew she wasn't that far along. She wasn't expecting to see a baby bump yet. Some women, she
knew, really didn't show, especially not with their
first one. And she hadn't been gaining weight.
Since she'd gotten pregnant, she'd actually lost
weight. That little accomplishment was due to
the fact that everything that she ate came back up
shortly thereafter.

Even water made her nauseous. And it didn't
happen just in the morning, but all day long.

At least that would keep her slim for the time
being. With a little bit of luck, no one needed to
know that she was in the family way, as they used
to say half a century ago, she thought. And in a
way, she supposed, it was a true assessment. This
baby represented the only family she had, and
most likely would ever have.

Still looking at herself critically, Elizabeth
turned left, then right, then left again and this time
moved ever so slowly to the right.

Not a thing, she silently declared in triumph.

As long as she looked like this, no one in their
right mind would think that she was pregnant, so
at least that aspect of this whole nerve-racking
situation wasn't going to be a problem yet—and
perhaps, with any luck, it never would.

Now that she thought about it, there had been
a number of stories over the years about women

who gave birth whose parents or closest friends hadn't even known they were pregnant.

All she needed, Elizabeth told herself, was a little bit of luck—and loose clothing.

Elizabeth went to get her sweater out of the closet. She intended to get a little air before dinner. Her clothing, she couldn't help thinking as she opened the sliding door, looked lost in the cavernous walk-in closet. Landry had offered to lend her some of hers.

Elizabeth smiled to herself. While she'd acknowledged the offer as being very sweet, she tactfully pointed out that the younger woman was three inches taller than she was and her clothes just wouldn't fit right.

Elizabeth reached for her sweater, which she'd left hanging on a hook on the left side of the closet.

The sweater wasn't there.

Staring at the empty hook, she frowned. She'd hung her sweater up last night. She'd put it on the hook that was on the left-hand side. She specifically recalled that, because the left side was where that pretty padded pink hanger was.

The hanger was still there.

The sweater was not.

Was she losing her mind? Elizabeth wondered nervously, staring at the empty hook. Sweaters didn't just vanish or walk away of their own volition. Besides, she could have *sworn* that she'd put the sweater right there.

Now it wasn't anywhere.

Feeling edgy, Elizabeth looked carefully around the bedroom, just in case, but the sweater wasn't anywhere to be seen. She wasn't about to check around the house to see if it had gotten misplaced in one of the million other rooms that seemed to be in this house, because if she strayed off the beaten path that she had grown familiar with, she would be hopelessly lost.

If ever a house cried out for bread crumbs to be left behind, marking a path, it was this house.

A more important reason not to go looking for the sweater was that she wasn't the type to just haphazardly toss off and leave a sweater—or any item of clothing—wherever the urge to discard hit. She valued everything she owned and treated it accordingly.

A last-ditch effort had Elizabeth looking on the floor of the closet to see if perhaps the sweater might have just fallen off and gotten inexplicably tangled amid her rather meager wardrobe.

Nothing.

An eerie feeling of déjà vu passed over her as she recalled other things that hadn't been where she expected to find them.

The feeling that someone was touching her things, moving them around, reared its head again.

But why would someone take her sweater? It just didn't make any sense to her. The sweater was far from unique or expensive and she had a feeling that the women who lived here, including the humble, exceptionally gentle Landry, were used to a far better quality of clothing than what she owned.

No, it just didn't make any sense to her, she thought.

Just like those blocked calls that had been sporadically appearing on her cell phone. The phone rang incessantly until she either picked up or the call was sent to voice mail.

In any event, there was never anyone there on the other end. Or rather, there was never anyone there who spoke. But Elizabeth thought she did detect shallow breathing just before the connection was broken.

She had no idea what this was all about, but she suspected that someone, for whatever reason, was trying to drive her crazy—literally.

She was not about to take that drive, Elizabeth told herself firmly. She *wasn't*, she silently swore this time around.

With a shrug, Elizabeth decided she'd just forego the sweater. She didn't need it for her walk. It was winter, yes, but winter in San Diego was not like winter in Buffalo, New York. The winters here were chilly, she granted. Sometimes they were even downright cold, but it was Southern

California cold, not Northeast cold, and that made all the difference in the world.

If she did feel chilly once she was outside, she'd just walk a little faster and get back to her guest room/prison a little quicker, she told herself.

But right now, she needed the morale-boosting feeling that she was going beyond the walls of her protection and could actually just go for a simple walk around the Adair compound.

Changing into a pair of jeans and a light blue sweatshirt that had AdAir's logo on it, she slipped on a pair of sneakers and stopped to loosen the laces on them a little.

Her feet were swelling just a tiny bit.

The discovery bothered her.

She knew that some women complained about their feet and ankles swelling during their period of being the baby's walking incubator, and she didn't relish going through that.

Maybe it wouldn't get any worse than this, she thought as she rose back up to her feet.

And if her feet were the only thing that did swell, she told herself, she would be very happy.

About to go down the stairs, she looked down and saw that one of the laces had come undone again.

She did better with Velcro, Elizabeth thought critically. Some mother she was going to make, she upbraided herself. She couldn't even tie a proper bow on her sneakers.

Taking a deep breath as she strove for patience, Elizabeth bent down. She thought she detected a faint scent of perfume as she was retying the wayward laces. She'd smelled that just recently—but where?

Just as she was getting back up on her feet, Elizabeth thought she felt someone's hands dead center on her back. The next second she was flying down the stairs—and not of her own volition.

Remembering something she had once read in a magazine article about fatal household accidents, she tucked herself into a ball as much as she could. She felt as though she was tumbling down the stairs head over heels.

The scream was totally involuntary.

Whit was in another section of the house, talking to his brother. Since that faith-shaking discovery of the possible existence of another older sibling, Carson had done his best to try to locate the missing heir or to find some record of his death, if this Jackson was no longer alive.

So far, Carson had just been spinning his wheels, going nowhere.

Until he had conducted an in-depth search of their late father's bedroom. Specifically, of their late father's walk-in closet.

"There were a whole bunch of business papers in his safe," Carson continued.

"You know the combination of his safe?" Whit asked, surprised.

Carson gave a half-careless shrug as he answered, "No."

Whit looked at him, perplexed. "Then how—?"

"You pick things up as a marine," Carson told him evasively.

"Safecracking?" Whit asked incredulously.

"Better you don't know," his brother said, then went back to telling Whit what he'd found. "There wasn't anything of interest in his safe, but in the space that was blocked off just behind it, I found this."

"This" turned out to be an ordinary shoe box filled with candid photographs of an infant, either sleeping or smiling, as well as a handful of other items, such as a teething ring, a few articles of tiny clothing and a small lop-eared teddy bear.

Whit looked at them in wonder. "Who would have thought that our father had a softer side?" he marveled, taking out a couple of the pictures to look over. "Anything in here to give you a clue what happened to our so-called big brother?"

Carson shook his head. "Not that I can see, although if we ever find a likely candidate, that teething ring might give us some DNA to work with."

He looked at the teething ring. "Provided it wasn't washed before it was put into this box of treasures," he pointed out.

Just then, they heard the loud scream, instantly followed by a loud thud.

"What the hell was that?" Carson asked, jumping to his feet.

Whit was already racing for the door. "Elizabeth!" was all he said as he tore out.

It was over before she knew it.

The awful sound of her body hitting the steps as she went down the full flight still echoed in her brain. A sense of disbelief permeated all through her.

Elizabeth didn't get up immediately because she didn't want to know immediately.

Didn't want to know if anything had been broken in that frightening fall down the entire length of the staircase.

Less than a minute later, both the landing above her and the first floor began filling with household help as well as members of the family.

Sound traveled very well in this house, Elizabeth thought, just now realizing that she must have screamed when she felt herself falling.

The first one to reach her was Whit.

Upstairs with Carson when it happened, he all

but flew down the stairs. He was kneeling beside her now, extremely concerned.

"Elizabeth, Elizabeth, are you all right?" he wanted to know. When he'd found her, her eyes were shut. But they fluttered open now.

"I've been better," she quipped. The next second, she was trying to sit up. Trying and failing, because Whit's hands were holding her in place, not allowing her to budge. Frustration filled her. "Let me up, Whit," she requested, her voice shaking.

His hands remained on her shoulders. "You might have broken something."

"Fastest way to find out whether I did or not is by letting me get up," she told him. Without waiting for his verbal compliance, Elizabeth grabbed hold of his arm and pulled herself up into a sitting position. "So far, so good," she told Whit, then winced as she started to drag herself all the way up to her feet.

Again, she failed.

"Stay down," Whit ordered. "You just winced when you moved."

"I'm wincing because it hurts," she informed him, annoyed at herself for being so clumsy, for attracting undue attention to herself when she wanted to slide under the radar and figure out just what the hell was going on. "You try going down that flight of stairs and not feel like a tennis ball after a championship match played out in the hot sun."

"I see your point," Whit conceded. Getting up to his feet, he took her hand in his and coaxed, "Slowly, very slowly."

She humored him, although she wanted nothing more than to just pop up like a piece of well-done toast.

Whit watched her carefully, studying every movement as well as every expression that crossed her face. "Can you stand?" he asked her.

"Stand? Yes," Elizabeth answered and to prove that she could, she let go of Whit's hand and continued to stand on her own.

He nodded at this minor accomplishment. "How about walk. Can you walk?" he wanted to know.

Ever so slowly, Elizabeth tested that out, too. Her gait was a little off, but not nearly as bad as it could have been. She did what she could to hang on to the positive side, declaring, "I can walk."

"Good," he pronounced with a nod of his head, still watching her. "Then walk with me out the door. Carson—" he turned toward his brother "—pull the car around."

Elizabeth looked from Whit to his brother. "Are we going somewhere?" she wanted to know. Maybe he was taking her to AdAir Corp so that she could do the transfer to her laptop right there.

But wouldn't he tell her she needed her laptop with her? Something was off.

The next moment, she found out what.

"Yes," Whit answered, taking one minuscule step at a time so as not to tax her. "I'm taking you to the hospital."

"Hospital?" Elizabeth stopped the little bit of progress she was making. "I'm not sick."

"No," he agreed, "but you might be broken." He saw Carson driving up the winding driveway with his sports car.

"But I'm standing up!" Elizabeth protested, sweeping her hand down along her body to drive home her point.

"People have been known to stand on a broken leg or broken ankle or broken thigh—want me to go on?" he asked, looking into her eyes.

The man definitely had a way of getting to her, she thought. "You could, couldn't you?"

Rather than say yes, he threw more facts at her. "Or a broken big toe. That, however, can generally heal itself unless—"

Elizabeth held up her hand, surrendering in order to stop the flow of words. She had no idea he could talk even half that fast. The man had hidden talents. "Okay, you got me. I'll go."

"*We'll* go," he corrected her, stepping outside and holding the door open for her. He waited as she hobbled outside.

We'll go. He said we, *not* you.

Elizabeth savored the difference. It almost made falling down the stairs worth it, she thought.

The next moment, the little voice inside her suggested that perhaps she'd hit her head in the fall, as well.

Annoyed, Elizabeth shut down the voice. Leaning on Whit's arm, she made her way outside.

"What happened?" Whit asked her once they were in the car and he was driving to the hospital. "How did you fall down the stairs?"

It was on the tip of her tongue to say she thought that someone had pushed her. But that would only result in one of two things. Either he'd think that she was paranoid and creating unlikely scenarios in her head—after all, why would someone push her? Or, he would believe her and conclude—as she had—that someone in the house was responsible for her unexpected tumble. Most likely he'd start questioning everyone to find whoever did this and he'd wind up alienating a lot of people who he needed to have on his side.

So she murmured that she had tripped and hoped that would be the end of it.

She could see by the look on his face that he didn't believe her. But for now, he was letting it go.

Chapter 12

Some bodyguard he made, Whit thought angrily.

Waiting for the orderly to bring Elizabeth back from Radiology was making him grow increasingly restless and fidgety.

What was taking them so damn long?

He should have been more alert, he criticized himself. Granted, he couldn't have foreseen her being clumsy and taking a header down the stairs, but if he had been with her instead of talking to Carson about their so-far fruitless efforts to locate this mysterious missing older brother of theirs, he might have been able to make a grab for her and keep her from tumbling down the stairs.

Instead, he was stuck here, impotently waiting for Elizabeth's return and for answers.

Falling that way, Elizabeth could have seriously injured herself. She might have broken an arm or a leg. Or her neck.

Hell, he thought, closing his eyes as if to squeeze away the thought, she could have been killed—and under his watch.

She would have been safer rollerblading in freeway traffic than staying with him at the ranch, Whit thought bitterly.

Unable to remain seated after Elizabeth had been taken for tests, he paced around the small empty space. The orderly had taken her to be x-rayed while she was still on the hospital gurney, leaving behind only a chair and the instruments that measured her vital signs to occupy the space.

He'd been too lax, Whit silently lectured. Both about protecting her and about putting the screws to the police department to step up the search for his father's killer. He had the gnawing feeling that Elizabeth wouldn't be entirely safe until his father's killer was behind bars. But the police were getting nowhere with the investigation.

Maybe he should hire the services of a security firm. Or better still—

Whit abruptly stopped pacing as the drape that had been enclosed around Elizabeth's space for privacy was suddenly drawn back. The next moment, the orderly was maneuvering Elizabeth's bed back to its initial position—with Elizabeth in it.

"Hi," she murmured almost shyly, as if this was an impromptu meeting between them and he hadn't been slowly going out of his mind, waiting.

Whit immediately approached the orderly. "How is she?" he wanted to know.

"Still in one piece," Elizabeth said, speaking up.

"The doctor will be by shortly to speak to you," the orderly told him politely.

Just about at the end of his supply of patience, Whit asked irritably, "Didn't they tell you anything when they were finished taking X-rays?"

"I just take the gurneys out and then bring them back, sir," the stocky young man told him. There was an apologetic note in his voice. However, there was no more information forthcoming.

Dragging a hand through his hair, Whit blew out a breath as he turned toward Elizabeth. He assumed she was as much in the dark as he was. He didn't understand why she wasn't as frustrated as he was.

"Why do they have to treat everything as if it's some sort of a classified secret? Why can't they just speak plainly, answer a few logical questions? Tell us what's going on?" he asked, raising his voice so that it followed the orderly down the corridor.

"Maybe they think you won't feel like you've

gotten your money's worth if everything is resolved so quickly," Elizabeth suggested.

Whit looked at his watch. "We've been here
over two hours. That's not being resolved quickly
in anyone's book," he declared.

This wasn't getting him anywhere, he thought.
With effort, he calmed down. Dragging over the
chair he'd previously occupied, he set it next to
Elizabeth's gurney. Whit sat down again and took
her hand in his. "How's your head?" he wanted
to know.

She offered him a weak smile. "It still feels a
little sore and I still have a headache," she confessed. "But it's nothing major. Don't worry so
much," she urged.

Shifting gears, since there was nothing else
to occupy their time, Whit tried to ascertain *why*
she'd fallen down the stairs. "Did you trip on
something on one of the steps?"

She began to shake her head and found that it
instantly increased her headache. So she stopped
and answered quietly, "No."

"Did you make a misstep?" he offered. He knew
that sometimes people miscalculated the height
of a step and it threw them off as they put their
foot down.

"No. I hadn't started to go downstairs yet," she
told him. "I was tying my shoelaces just before—
just before it happened," she concluded hesitantly.

Whit frowned, taking in the information. "Then you weren't moving? I don't understand. How did you wind up falling down the stairs if you weren't moving? Did you faint?"

Elizabeth looked away. If she told him, she would be accusing someone in his family of trying to harm her, and she didn't want to do that. They'd taken her in. To accuse one of them of being responsible for this trip to the ER didn't seem right.

"Let's just drop it, please," she said, still avoiding any eye contact with Whit.

He had no intentions of dropping this. He intended to get to the bottom of it. "No. I want to know. If you tripped over your own feet, well, these things happen. I won't hold it against you. I—"

She knew she should just let it go at this, but it bothered her, being painted as a klutz. More than that, it bothered her to lie to him.

"No, I *didn't* trip over my own feet," she informed him.

He'd run out of guesses. "Then how did you wind up falling down the stairs?" Whit wanted to know.

Elizabeth opened and closed her mouth twice before finally finding the words to say, "I think I might have been pushed."

Elizabeth saw his face turn pale and his expression grow instantly very somber.

Elizabeth was making a very serious accusation, he thought. He'd known her to be nothing but truthful in all his dealings with her, but he found it difficult to imagine what she was saying now was actually true.

"What makes you say that?" he wanted to know, his voice deadly still.

She should never have said anything, Elizabeth thought. But now that she had, she had to see this through. "Because just before I tumbled down the stairs, I felt something."

"Felt something," he repeated, trying to make sense out of what she was telling him. What did that even mean? What was she trying to say? "What kind of something?" Whit wanted to know.

Elizabeth took a deep breath, bracing herself. The deep breath, in turn, reminded her of the scent she'd thought she detected just before her fall.

"I thought I felt someone's hands on my back... giving me a shove," she told him hesitantly. "Look, I didn't want to come here at all. Can't we just leave and go home? I haven't broken anything. They would have already put some part of me into a cast if that was the case. Please, let's just leave," she begged.

"Can't," he answered matter-of-factly. "The ER physician has to sign you out before you can go," he reminded her.

That wasn't strictly true. "I can sign myself out," she told him.

"That wouldn't be advisable," Whit countered.

There was silence between them for a moment, a heavy silence that didn't sit well with either one of them. It made Whit uncomfortable.

"What aren't you telling me?" he asked Elizabeth out of the blue.

She almost jumped at the sound of his voice. If her nerves had been any more taut, they could have doubled as violin strings.

"What do you mean?" she asked, trying very hard to look innocent. It only succeeded in making her appear more guilty.

Was he asking her about the baby? Had he somehow found out that she was carrying his child? But how?

"I can see it in your eyes. There's something else. Do you *know* who pushed you?"

He was still talking about the so-called accident. She felt a wave of relief wash over her. He didn't know. And she was going to keep it that way for as long as possible.

"I didn't see anyone," she answered.

"That's not what I asked," Whit pointed out. "I asked if you knew who did this to you." He leaned in a little closer, doing his best not to react to her but keep his mind focused on the subject. "You do know, don't you?" he asked. Her body language told him he'd guessed right. "Elizabeth, tell me who it is. Who pushed you down the stairs?"

She raised her chin almost defiantly. "Like I said, I didn't see anyone."

His eyes pinned her down, leaving her no room to squirm. "But?"

He wasn't going to stop asking questions until she told him what he wanted to hear, Elizabeth thought. "But I think I might have detected a scent."

"What kind of a scent?" he asked. "Was it body odor, or—"

Her stomach was feeling queasy again. She didn't want him going over a list of pungent smells. It would only make her more nauseous.

"Perfume. Expensive perfume," she added, staring down at the thin cotton cover on the gurney.

"You might have caught a whiff of your own perfume," he told her.

God knew that he did often enough. There was something very arousing about the scent she wore. When it filled his head, it made him want to drop to his knees in surrender, as long as she was the person he was surrendering to.

But Elizabeth shook her head—instantly regretting the movement. "You don't smell your own cologne or perfume. After a very short while, you become completely desensitized to it."

"Then whose—?" It hit him like the proverbial ton of bricks. His sister didn't wear perfume. But someone else in the family did. "Mother's," he declared. "You smelled my mother's perfume, didn't you?"

Accusing his mother of a deed like that would instantly turn her into the enemy, she thought. She didn't want to be his enemy.

"Whit, she might have just passed by a minute before the other person who pushed me did. You said yourself that she never ventures to your side of the hacienda."

She was making excuses for his mother, but now that her name was on the table, Whit could see his mother being capable of doing something so cold and detached. However, she would need a reason, no matter how strange it might sound to the rest of them.

Whit looked at Elizabeth. "Is there something going on or that has gone down between the two of you that you're not telling me?"

"No, nothing. I swear," she told him with feeling. "You know every detail of my boring life," Elizabeth assured him.

He shook his head. No matter how he looked at it, it wasn't making any sense. "Then I don't—"

Just then, the ER physician, a Dr. A. Walker, came in, a bright, warm smile on his face.

"Well, good news, you two," Dr. Walker said. "There's no evidence of a concussion, nor do you have any hairline fractures that we can find. Just some minor bruising, and you'll be experiencing aches and pains for probably the next three days or so. Other than that, you're good to go."

Elizabeth sighed, incredibly relieved. "Thank you, Doctor."

"No need to thank me. I'm just the messenger, nothing more." He was about to leave when he suddenly remembered what he saw as the most important detail of all. "Oh, and by the way, despite that tumble, your baby's fine, too. I'd say you were one lucky lady," the doctor pronounced. "I'm signing your papers and you're free to go. Wish everyone who came in here could be as fortunate as you."

With that, the doctor made his exit.

She could feel Whit's scrutiny as if it was a physical thing.

Looking at him, Elizabeth could almost *see* him literally closing up again.

Her mind began to race around, searching for a way to communicate with him, to explain why she'd withheld this all-important piece of information from him.

Where did she begin?

How did she start?

"Whit—" she began.

"You'd better get dressed," he told her crisply. "I'll wait for you outside."

She stared numbly at the white curtain after he pulled it closed behind him.

This was the worst possible thing that could have happened, she thought, desperate for a way to fix this, to make it all go away and replay itself differently.

Fighting tears, she got dressed, hardly remembering the process once it was over.

It was all she could do to remember to keep breathing.

"I know you're angry," Elizabeth began once they were out of the hospital and in his car. She knew that if she didn't say something to explain herself and her actions, Whit wasn't going to say a word the entire trip back to the ranch.

"Why should I be angry?" Whit countered coldly. "You're a grown woman, what you do— and with who—is your own business. All that time you worked late with my father, it was really just inevitable. My father was a good-looking man and lonely, from what I gather. You're a beautiful woman, so naturally—"

"Wait, what?" she cried, trying to make sense out of what he was saying to her. She definitely didn't like what she was coming up with. What Whit was suggesting not only horrified her, it turned her stomach, as well. "You think— Are you—" She tried to compose herself but it was nearly impossible. "This isn't your father's baby," she spat out, upset and offended that he'd even think such a terrible thing.

"You don't have to deny it," he told her calmly, still looking straight ahead rather than at her.

As far as he was concerned, she was just a disembodied voice, another one of his father's women who also worked for the company. She just happened to be smarter than most of the women his father had interacted with, which was why he'd made her his executive assistant. Obviously his father hadn't held himself up to any high moral standard, but the company was another matter entirely. Promotions were earned, not handed out in exchange for sexual favors.

That didn't help soothe his wounded feelings.

Whit struggled to contain his anger, his outrage. He'd always wanted to share things with his father, but the same women never numbered among those things.

"I do if it's not true," she told him, anger infusing her every word. "I don't know what it is you think me capable of, but you are the *only* man I have slept with since my junior year in college. That experience was so not memorable that I didn't want to go out with another guy for the rest of my life. That I wound up in bed with you that night was just the result of a whole bunch of different factors choosing that moment to come together."

Whit abruptly pulled over to the side of the road and turned off the engine. "Let me get this straight. Are you telling me that this baby you're carrying is actually *mine*?"

She didn't know if that was denial in his voice or awe. "Would you like me to explain it using hand puppets?" she offered, the tension bubbling within her bringing a wave of sarcasm to the surface.

He stared at her. She was telling him the truth. It was too easy to do a DNA test these days for her to think she could get away with a lie.

That left him with one glaring question. "Why didn't you tell me? The only reason I ever assumed it was someone else's is because if the baby really was mine, I would have expected you to come to me."

"I'm your father's executive assistant. I'm also from the wrong side of the tracks. You're the vice president of a hugely successful cell phone service provider. Do the math. Telling you that our one night together yielded a tiny dividend would sound like a shakedown. And it's not," she said firmly, just so there was no misunderstanding. "I don't want anything from you."

He looked at her as if he didn't understand her logic. "But that's my baby," he repeated.

Maybe he thought she was trying to retain exclusive rights to the baby and bar him from ever seeing the child. That wasn't her intent. "You can see him—or her—anytime you want."

That wasn't enough—not by a long shot. He wasn't a man who shirked his responsibilities, and he wanted to do right by this child. "I want the baby to have my last name."

That was no problem, she thought. "That can be arranged. It'll be entered on the birth certificate," she promised.

But Whit shook his head, frowning. "That's not enough."

"We can have the birth certificate laminated," she answered flippantly.

His eyes pinned her down. "I want to do the right thing."

He sounded like someone straight out of the '60s, she thought. "There is no right or wrong thing in this case," she informed him.

He wasn't accepting that. "There is in my world. We'll get married," he told her in a no-nonsense tone of voice. "It'll take me a little while to set everything in motion, but it can be—"

"Stop. Stop!" Elizabeth shouted. His thoughts coming to a grinding halt, Whit looked at her, caught off guard and surprised. "Aren't you listening?" she demanded angrily. "I don't want anything from you. I never did. You're not obligated to do anything."

That was not the way he saw it. "It's my baby

and my child deserves to have a family. That means a mother and father who will be there for him, night and day."

That sounded very idyllic—except for one very important thing he forgot to mention. "And love? Does love enter into it?" she wanted to know.

"Of course. I already love him—or her," Whit said, and he knew that it was true. He did. These past few minutes, when he'd realized that there was a child waiting to be born, a child that was part his, a transformation had occurred within him.

He didn't get it, did he? "I'm talking about me, Whit. The only reason in this world to get married is love. Do you love me?" she asked pointedly.

The silence within the car was deafening—and thus soul destroying.

Chapter 13

Putting his feelings into words did not come easily for Whit. For the most part, he *had* no feelings that he thought needed to be expressed.

But in this particular instance, because there was a child to think of, he did his best to try to make Elizabeth understand what was going on within him.

"If I *could* love anyone, Elizabeth, it would be you," Whit told her. Each word he uttered stood alone, like an awkward soldier unschooled in basic social graces.

Elizabeth looked at him. Was that *it*? Was that all he had to say? Did he think that rather backhanded apology was supposed to satisfy her? Make her relent her position, agree to settle for less than love and marry him?

If *that* was what he thought, then Whit was in for a surprise, Elizabeth silently predicted.

She didn't ask for much, but she did ask for—actually, *demand*—this. That he only marry her if he loved her. Because if he *didn't* love her, then they weren't going to get married at all. She was not about to accept a sham of a marriage, no matter how good Whit thought his reason for going through with it was.

"My turn to say 'not enough,'" Elizabeth told him in a quiet, controlled voice.

"I'm being honest with you," Whit told her, his frustration and helplessness mounting. "I don't know if I'm actually *capable* of love, Elizabeth," he confessed. "I've got nothing to base it on, no examples to follow. My parents' marriage didn't exactly merit the *Good Housekeeping* seal of approval. Most of the time, if they spoke at all, it was to say hurtful, cutting things—unless they were in public," he amended. "Then it was all sweetness and light. They put on a decent enough show, but once they were home, they went back to their separate corners, their separate lives." Whit told her truthfully, "I don't even have a clue what goes into making a good relationship."

He made it sound as if there was some prefabricated formula out on the market. "Marriage isn't something that comes out of a box with assembly instructions. You don't build a marriage like you build make-believe castles using kids' building blocks," she insisted. "A successful marriage takes constant work and above all, it's something that comes from within. From your heart. You either feel it—or you don't."

Elizabeth looked at him for a long moment, giving Whit every opportunity to deny what she was about to say and set her straight.

But he didn't.

"And you," she concluded with a heavy heart, "obviously don't."

"So you're turning me down?" Whit asked incredulously. She knew what he was worth, give or take a couple of million. He'd thought that alone would win her over. It would win over a lot of women he knew. But then, Elizabeth wasn't like *any* other woman he knew. "You're turning down my marriage proposal?"

This was crazy, she thought. Absolutely crazy. There was nothing in the *world* she would have wanted more than to marry him—but only under the right conditions. And right now, they weren't right. They weren't right at all.

"I never thought I'd ever hear myself say this, but yes, I'm turning down your marriage proposal."

Maybe that fall *had* addled her brain, Whit

thought, unable to understand why she would turn him down—if for no other reason then to secure the child's future. "Elizabeth—"

"Please take me home," she requested, gesturing toward the path that lay in front of his car. "I think I'd like to get some rest now, like the ER doctor suggested."

"This isn't over," Whit told her stoically, starting up his car again.

"No," she agreed quietly, looking down at her still very flat abdomen, "it's not."

"I'd like to keep this just between us for a while," Elizabeth said as Whit pulled up in front of his family's house. When he looked at her, one eyebrow arched in a silent query, she specified, "You know, the part about the baby."

Did she really think that she could keep her pregnancy a secret? Didn't she realize that it was just a matter of time?

"That's not exactly something that you can hide indefinitely," he told her, pulling up the hand brake and turning the engine off.

Her eyes locked with his. "You're assuming that I'm going to be living at the ranch from here on in, and I'm not."

This point was nonnegotiable as far as he was concerned. "You are as long as my father's killer is out there," he informed her. There was no arguing with his tone of voice.

She ached and was more than weary. Too weary to argue with Whit about this now. But she would later. She wasn't about to become a prisoner in this house. She really liked Landry, and Carson was very likable, as well. The household staff treated her not just politely but with kindness. If they were the only ones living here, there would be no problem. But being around Whit, wanting him to love her and knowing that he didn't—or couldn't—that was asking just too much of her. Everyone had a limit and that was definitely hers.

She'd iron all this out later, when she was more up to it, Elizabeth told herself as she slowly eased herself out of the car.

Whit had already rounded the sports car and was at her side, waiting. He took her elbow, determined to help her up the steps.

Elizabeth pulled her arm back. "Don't worry, I can manage. I'm not going to fall down—or up—every step I encounter."

"Humor me," Whit told her tersely. Taking her arm again, he escorted her to the front door.

It seemed to Elizabeth that the moment they walked into the house, people converged from all directions, gathering around them, firing questions.

The household help seemed just as concerned as Carson and Landry appeared to be.

Carson raised his voice slightly to be heard above the others. "Are you all right?"

Landry came to her other side. "Did you break anything?" she wanted to know, her eyes sweeping over Elizabeth, obviously looking for a cast of some sort.

"Why aren't you in the hospital for observation?" Carson wanted to know.

"She's fine," Whit told his siblings authoritatively, thinking to satisfy their questions as well as the questions coming from some of the staff members who were showing their concern. It was obvious to him that during her short stay here, Elizabeth had touched lives and made quite an impression. He went on to tell them, "There's nothing broken or fractured and she didn't want to stay overnight for any further observation." His mouth curved slightly as he said, "It was all they could do to keep her there long enough for X-rays to be taken."

It was at that moment that Patsy regally swept into the gathering, cutting a path for herself with every step she took. Her attention was clearly fixed on Elizabeth.

"Perhaps you should have stayed at the hospital overnight, dear. We all know that tests aren't always accurate. Perhaps they missed something important." Whit's mother slowly circled her.

The image of a white tiger toying with its prey seemed to burn itself into Elizabeth's brain.

"You *do* look very shaken up and pale, dear. A little extra time in a hospital bed might be just what you needed. I would cover the cost, of course, since you fell down stairs that were in my house," Patsy informed her grandly.

"She's an adult, Mother," Whit pointed out, struggling to keep his temper in check. Since his father's murder, he found himself growing less and less tolerant these days. "And quite capable of making up her own mind."

"I'm sure she is. No one said she wasn't," Patsy replied loftily with a dismissive wave of her hand. "Just, sometimes, when you get banged around the way Elizabeth clearly did, you're not always capable of clear thinking. I was just trying to be helpful," Patsy said, smiling up into her house-guest's face.

"I appreciate that," Elizabeth said, doing her best not to clench her teeth.

As she said the words, Elizabeth winced inwardly. Now she was playing games, just like Patsy was, saying things she didn't mean.

But there was more. Being in the woman's company for even an instant had convinced her that Whit's mother was the one who'd pushed her. She couldn't be mistaken about that perfume. No one else here wore it or anything close to it. Not Landry and certainly not any of the female household staff.

She slanted a glance toward Patsy. Just why did the woman hate her so much? Was it just the way she reacted to every woman whose path had crossed the late Reginald Adair's, or was there something more personal involved here? She had no way of knowing.

Elizabeth's head began to hurt again.

"If you don't mind, I think I'll just go to my room and lie down for a while," Elizabeth said to the group in general and to Whit specifically.

"*Excellent* idea," Patsy declared, beaming at her with satisfaction as if she had just beaten her in a tricky chess maneuver. "You go right ahead and do that, dear. And let me know if you need anything from the staff, anything at all," she added, playing the benevolent hostess up to the hilt.

"I will," Elizabeth heard herself saying just as she walked away from the poisonous woman.

She did *not* belong here, Elizabeth thought a little while later. Maybe Whit meant well, wanting to watch over her until whoever had killed his father was caught. But all things considered, she didn't think she was going to fare all that well here if she was forced to stay. There were a number of reasons she felt that way, not to mention that his mother seemed to really have it in for her, and who knew what else the woman was capable of doing?

Her safest bet was to get her things together as soon as possible and to leave—she'd sneak out in the middle of the night if she had to, Elizabeth decided. The safety of her baby came above all else and she was afraid that the baby wasn't safe here.

The knock on her door had Elizabeth stiffening and all but jumping out of her skin.

Relax, Lizzy. The witch doesn't know how to read minds.

The second knock had her responding, "Yes?" as she looked around the room for something to use as a weapon—just in case she needed to defend herself.

Rather than someone talking to her through the door, she saw the guest room door opening. Her heart sped up tenfold. The next moment, she realized that it was Whit—and he was carrying a tray.

"I thought you might be hungry. As far as I can remember, you didn't have lunch *or* dinner today," he told her, carrying the tray over to a side table.

He was right, she hadn't eaten, but food was the very last thing on her mind right now.

"You didn't have to do this," she told him, indicating the tray. "I know where the kitchen is."

Whit drew the table over to her bed for her convenience. "Knowing where it is and going there are two separate things. I can't have you starving to death just because you're stubborn."

"I'm not hungry." It was a lie. Now that she

gave it some thought, she realized that she actually *was* hungry. But she was also going through some major conflicting feelings.

And Whit definitely figured into all of them.

"Then do it to keep your strength up—for the baby's sake," he coaxed.

She opened her mouth to argue and to tell him that he fought dirty. But Whit really was making sense. To oppose him in this case made her seem unreasonable and combative for its own sake.

With a shrug, she gave in.

"Mind if I stay?" he asked her. "I can go if you want me to," he added so she wouldn't think he was just being rhetorical, asking her if she minded his presence. He didn't want her to feel as if he was forcing his company on her.

"No, that's all right," Elizabeth quickly conceded. "You can stay." She looked at the tray of food he'd brought in for her. "You can help me finish this."

"You need help?" Whit asked, amazed. "There's hardly anything here," he pointed out. And, in his estimation, thinking like a man with a man's appetite, there wasn't. "A dove would be hard-pressed to sustain itself on just this."

"A dove, huh?" That struck her as an odd choice for a comparison. "Why a dove?" she wanted to know.

"First thing that came to mind." He shrugged.

"A dove is pretty, gentle, elegant when it flies." He looked at her. "There're a lot of similarities between the two of you."

"I'm just a little larger," she said wryly.

"Just a little," he agreed.

"And I don't fly," she added, an amused smile curving the corners of her mouth.

"Minor detail," he replied.

Silence ensued for a couple of beats, and then Whit said what had been on his mind ever since he'd found out about his unborn child. "I'm glad you never slept with my father."

"You actually thought that I had?" Elizabeth questioned, both surprised and upset that he had even entertained such a thought. His mother was just a vicious, exceedingly jealous person, but he should have known better. That he didn't hurt her.

"Why?" she wanted to know. "Did you think so little of me?"

"No, just the opposite," Whit was quick to assure her. "The first time I saw you, you were so regal-looking, you all but melted my knees. I wasn't sure if I would be able to walk away."

The words were very pretty—she hadn't thought him capable of giving voice to something like that—but it still didn't change the way things were. "You hardly talked to me," she reminded him.

In five years, Whit had never asked her a single personal question. And when they did talk, it was always about work. Had that fateful night in Nevada not happened, she would have sworn that he wouldn't have been able to pick her out of a lineup.

"Because I thought you and my father—" Whit stopped, struggling to find the right words to use, words that would explain but not offend. He tried again. "I couldn't see him not wanting you. You were everything he always valued in a woman. You were—and are—beautiful, smart and extremely sharp."

Again, lovely adjectives, but at bottom was an insult he was attempting to distract her from recognizing. "And you thought that all your father had to do was beckon and I'd fall into bed with him?"

"Not in those words, but—" He was definitely struggling with this explanation. It just wasn't coming out right. "That would be the end result, yes," Whit conceded.

"Well, I didn't fall into bed with him, not even once," she replied primly. "I wouldn't. And I think he knew that, because your father never propositioned me." She smiled to herself as she thought over her work environment. "I think he valued my brain more than my looks."

But Whit wasn't ready to let this go just yet. They'd gone this far with it, he wanted to go all the way. "And if he *had* propositioned you?"

Her eyes met his. Hers had a look of angry defiance in them. "I still wouldn't have gone to bed with him. I have to *feel* something before I make love with a man," she informed Whit.

"But you went to bed with me," Whit reminded her. There'd been no in-depth conversation, no protestations of feelings or declarations of love. Not even fleetingly. They had talked over dinner—a fairly liquid dinner—and then they'd made love as if it were the most natural thing in the world.

She looked down at her tray. The little bit of food he had brought her was almost all gone. She hardly remembered eating it.

"I refer you to my last statement," she told him quietly. Looking up, she saw that Whit appeared somewhat puzzled. "In case you weren't paying attention, I said that I have to *feel* something for the person I'm going to bed with. Something that amounts to a lot more than a whim, or because there's nothing interesting on any of the cable channels," she informed Whit cryptically. "I'm finished," she announced.

A sense of anxiety surged through him. Was she saying she was finished with him? With the family? With remaining here, under his roof? Or was she saying something even more ominous?

"What?" he pressed, lost. "What are you finished with?"

"Eating," she supplied, indicating the tray. "I'm finished eating. You can bring the tray back to the kitchen if you like. Or leave it here and I'll take it there in the morning."

She wasn't sure why, but her words suddenly felt rather heavy, weighing down her tongue, sticking to the roof of her mouth as she uttered them.

Maybe it had to do with the look in his eyes. He was looking at her as if he had never really seen her before this moment.

Whit moved the tray and the table under it off to the side. Instead of carrying the tray out as she'd suggested, Whit moved in closer, occupying the space that had been taken up by the side table a moment ago.

"I'm sorry," he told her, his voice low, sensual.

Her heart rate was beginning to speed up. She could feel it as it started to race. His eyes were now locked with hers.

"For what?" she asked.

"That I can't be what you want me to be. If I could, I would."

This was tearing at her heart, but she didn't give in because she *knew* there was more to be had than what he believed there was. *Everyone* could feel love—they just had to *want* to feel it.

"If you wanted to be," Elizabeth informed him, "you would be. We are all masters of our own destinies," she told him quietly. "Even if we don't think we are."

Whit took her chin in his hand, looking into her eyes. Thinking just how beautiful she was.

There was a glow to her, he realized. Had pending motherhood done that?

Or was it just his own desire that painted her in golden hues?

He didn't know and right now, it didn't really matter. All that mattered was this all-consuming ache for her that he felt inside of him. He needed to appease it, to silence it. To make it go away.

Whit brought his lips down on hers.

Elizabeth's breath caught in her throat. She didn't pull away.

Chapter 14

The little voice in her head that was screaming "Mayday" was growing fainter and fainter, drowned out by the triple beat of her heart as well as suppressed by the size of her desire.

Elizabeth hadn't really known how much she'd wanted this—or how much she really wanted *him*—until Whit had come to her room and kissed her like this.

The last time he'd kissed her, she had felt aroused, but that surging feeling had been cut short and she'd known that nothing was going to come of it.

Nothing *should* have come from it.

There was no such sensation now.

Now she had a very strong feeling that Whit would make love with her unless she herself put a stop to it. It was all up to her how this would go— or didn't go. All completely in her hands.

Elizabeth was well aware of that.

The first time they had made love, it had practically been a matter of spontaneous combustion.

But even then she'd known that if she wanted it to go no further, to stop before they became totally, hopelessly intimate, Whit would have stopped. He was not the type of man who forced himself on a woman, not the type of man who would claim that once uncorked, the champagne bottle could not be recorked and put away, seemingly intact.

Elizabeth was not sure of many things in this life, but she would have bet her soul on that.

This time, just as on that very fateful night, she had no desire to stop, no desire to step away from the center of all this passion and pretend nothing was going on.

Whit might not love her, she conceded, but right now, he wanted to make love *to* her and with her. Right now, because of the way she ached inside, the way she suddenly, desperately wanted him, she would settle for that.

If he couldn't love her, she was willing, just this one last time, to go that route. Accepting his marriage proposal would be equivalent to living an endless lie, but making love with him, that was living in the moment. And right now, all that counted to her was the moment.

Whit had forgotten just how very sweet her lips could taste. Forgotten just how much she could stir him up with the slightest touch of her hand.

His head was spinning and he could feel his gut twisting almost into a knot for want of her. He *wanted* to make love with her.

The forbidden fruit label had been peeled off. She wasn't forbidden to him anymore. Elizabeth hadn't been his father's mistress.

She denied ever having slept with his father, and he believed her. Heaven help him, he believed her. Whether it was because he wanted to so badly or because he trusted her not to lie, he wasn't really able to say. But the end result was that he felt Elizabeth was telling the truth when she said she had never been one of his father's playthings.

The relief was enormous.

Knowing that she had never graced his father's bed put an entirely new spin on what was happening between them. He wasn't making love with one of his father's leftovers. Whatever their so-called relationship or dalliance was, wherever it might lead or not lead, it belonged to them alone, untainted by his father's fingerprints.

Whit had always hated existing beneath his father's shadow. He was his own man.

The kiss between them heated up almost instantly.

One moment, Whit was just deepening the kiss, the next he had gently pushed her back against her bed, moving with her.

Continuing the kiss.

His lips sealed to hers, Whit found himself putting his entire being into that kiss, stoking the fire that was just beneath.

His hands began to roam almost possessively over her body, touching, caressing, claiming. And all the while he was doing that, his clever fingers were divesting Elizabeth of the nightshirt she'd slipped on.

Since she'd intended on going to bed, she had nothing on beneath the nightshirt. There were no more barriers to keep him from her.

There was just her bare skin.

The instant his fingertips glided along the velvet-soft skin, he could feel his loins quickening, could feel his own breath turning almost solid in his lungs.

The feel of her skin set his own on fire. He knew he should be backing away. She'd turned down his proposal, which meant she didn't want to be married to him. At the very least, he should have been insulted instead of aching for her this way.

Common sense as well as a sense of morality told him he shouldn't be doing this, and yet, something within him felt it would curl up and die if he didn't.

So he kissed her.

Over and over again, he kissed her. Kissed her lips, the sides of her neck, the swell of her breasts and beyond.

Each moment fed on the next, making him bolder. Making him yearn.

Tugging the nightshirt from her body, he let it slide off the bed and onto the floor. He was otherwise occupied. Hardly able to catch his breath— her nearly perfect body was making it increasingly difficult for him to breathe—he pressed his lips to Elizabeth's bare shoulders, then created a damp trail of kisses that led down to her navel and then farther than that.

Every part of her was his.

Elizabeth pulled frantically on his shirt, desperate to eliminate the barrier it provided.

Pausing for just a moment, Whit raised his arms, allowing her to drag his shirt off his torso.

Before he could resume what he was doing, she'd pushed the button free of its confining hole on his trousers. After that, the trousers disappeared, removed via a joint effort.

She was about to push him down on the bed, to have her turn at raining kisses up and down all along his torso, but Whit was faster than she was. Before she knew it, she was the one whose back was against the comforter while Whit went back to what he'd been doing: claiming every inch of her body by branding her with his mouth and his tongue and nipping her with his teeth.

And Elizabeth reveled in it. She twisted and turned beneath him, as much to absorb the sensations as to give him new areas to make his own.

When he got down to the very core of her, the ecstasy was almost too much for her to bear. Elizabeth had to bite down hard on her lower lip to keep from crying out. Whit had brought her up to a climax before she even realized what he was doing.

The first climax flowered into another and then another, just like an endless, ever-widening fireworks display across the sky on the Fourth of July.

Arching her back to try and absorb every nuance, every last bit of the wondrous sensation rippling all through her like a hundred small earthquakes, she dug her fingertips into his shoulders.

The next second, with her last ounce of available strength, she dragged him up until his face was level with hers.

Their bodies were aligned.

Aware that he was on borrowed time and that he was not going to be able to hold out indefinitely, Whit positioned himself over her and then, his eyes once more on hers, their hands linked above her head, he entered her, claiming a woman who was already his—or at least she had been during that one magical, memorable night they'd shared.

He wished with all his heart that he could give her what she wanted—because it was what he would have wanted as well. But a man knew his own limitations, and Whit was convinced that this was his.

He couldn't love—he could only *want* to love.

The exception was his unborn child. He could already feel love growing and multiplying within his heart for the child he had yet to meet.

Just like your father, a voice echoed in his head. He'd quickly gone through that box of baby things that Carson had found in their father's closet. He'd read a few entries in a diary that his father wrote in sporadically, apparently only when the mood moved him. In one entry he mentioned being surprised that he could care so much for someone so tiny and helpless. Someone who couldn't communicate a single word but who could somehow light up his soul.

That was as close as he was going to come to love himself, Whit thought as he made love with Elizabeth. He wished that it was enough for her, because he knew, in absence of the teeth-jarring real thing, that he could live with that.

The urgency within him grew to such proportions, it left not a drop of room for anything else. Certainly not any coherent thoughts.

The tempo quickened as he and Elizabeth raced together for that final second's embrace, and to celebrate the all-encompassing final surge that promised to capture both of them and hold them in its delicious, viselike grip.

But even as it occurred, as that wondrous sensation pervaded all through them, it began to dissolve, backing away from them slowly, leaving a soft sense of euphoria in its wake.

Eventually, even that was gone.

Opening his eyes, Whit looked at her for a long-drawn-out moment, then brushed back some of her hair from her face.

Elizabeth's eyes fluttered open.

She wasn't asleep after all, Whit thought. For a moment, she'd been so still, he was certain she had drifted off to sleep.

"Sorry," he told her—a blanket apology for anything she might feel merited one. "I guess I just got carried away."

How could he make love to her like that, make her feel as if she could *fly* over anything, and not love her? It didn't make sense to her.

"Yeah, I guess we both did," she replied, her voice so low he could barely hear it.

Raising himself up on one elbow, Whit turned

his body in to hers, the movement totally unself-conscious. He looked at her for a long, long moment.

She had been incredibly flexible, all but blowing him away.

"I guess you really don't have any stress fractures," he concluded, only half teasing her. "You didn't wince once."

"You didn't exactly leave much room for wincing. That was a full-scale attack," she told him—but she was smiling as she said it.

"I like being thorough." And then his smile faded just a touch as he asked, "I didn't hurt you, did I?"

She tried to keep a straight face, but in the end, she failed. "It's a little late for concern, don't you think?"

"Better late than never," he countered and then he gently touched her face. "If you need anything, anything at all, you'll tell me, right?"

He was talking about meeting his obligations as a father, she thought. "You mean if I need anything for the baby, right?"

"No, anything at all," he emphasized. "That means the baby *and* you. I want you to let me know. If you won't marry me, well, that's your decision, I guess. But I still want to take care of you and the baby."

This was killing her, she thought. He was a good man with good intentions and maybe just too honest for *her* own good. When he'd proposed to her, he hadn't needed to tell her that he couldn't love her. Granted, she would have undoubtedly figured it out on her own, but not all that quickly, especially not if he made love with her like this.

Even knowing what she did about the fact that his feelings were paralyzed, she'd been completely blown away by his lovemaking.

Could a man make love like that and still not *feel* anything at all?

He was looking at her, waiting for an answer— she could see it in his eyes.

"Yes, I'd tell you," she said.

What else *could* she say? She didn't want his money, especially not in lieu of his love. But she wasn't exactly dressed for a long-drawn-out debate on the subject.

She wasn't even dressed for a short discussion, she thought, suddenly amused at the whole situation. Lovemaking had left her feeling rather giddy and upbeat.

Whit searched her face for some sign that she was telling the truth. Her expression was unreadable. "You're sure?" he asked.

God help her, she was lying, she thought. But it was a necessary lie, to keep everything from just exploding and going haywire. To keep from wounding him, although why she should care about his feelings when he obviously didn't care about hers was beyond her right now.

"I'm sure," she replied.

He smiled at her then, and the next moment, cupping her cheek and tilting her head ever so slightly, he kissed her.

It was supposed to be a kiss to seal the bargain, perhaps even to say "thank you." But it didn't turn out that way.

He discovered that the taste of her mouth was utterly irresistible to him no matter how many times he kissed her—or maybe *because* of all the times he'd kissed her.

One kiss led to another as sure as the sun rose in the east and bedded down in the west. This time was no different.

There it went again, Elizabeth thought. Her heart was taking off as if they hadn't just spent the last forty-five minutes making wild, passionate love with one another.

What was she, insatiable? Elizabeth silently demanded. How was she going to reconcile all this with her feelings about his stand? She would think about that later, Elizabeth told herself.

Tomorrow.

Whenever.

Right now, she didn't want to think, even though that was the way she was normally wired. Right now, all she wanted to do—again—was feel. And he made her feel glorious.

Beautiful.

Despite everything, despite her attacks of lack of confidence, he made her feel like the most beautiful and desirable creature on earth.

That had never happened to her before and she wanted to hold on to that feeling for as long as she could. But beneath it all, she also knew she had to be logical.

"Won't someone come looking for you?" she asked Whit.

The last thing she wanted was to have someone come knocking on her door with Whit lying naked in her bed. She knew without asking that he wouldn't suddenly jump up and hide in the closet to avoid detection. He would remain just where he was, and she wasn't sure if she was up for that and all the things that such a discovery would cause to rain down on both of them.

"It's late," Whit reminded her. "And it's not like I have a keeper—or that anyone even really cares where I am."

He began to kiss her again, but she was quicker and placed her index finger against his lips, stopping him. She wasn't finished making her point.

"Your father was murdered and someone— possibly the same person as the one who murdered your father—pushed me down the stairs. I'd say that's plenty cause for your family to worry about you if you're not where you're supposed to be."

"That's just it," he told her, rolling her onto her back in one quick movement with his body looming over hers. "I'm not supposed to be any particular place. And there are a hell of a lot of places in this house that I *could* be."

Although, Whit had to silently admit, Carson would probably figure out that if he wasn't in his room and his car was still on the property, he would be here, in Elizabeth's room.

He decided he didn't need to share that with her, especially since he didn't know just how she would react to it.

"Now if you'd like me to stop, all you have to do is say so," he told her, giving her the option to do just that. He waited a beat, then two, but she didn't say anything. "Well?" he asked.

"I'm not saying so," she told him, an almost impish smile on her face.

She knew in her heart that tonight was an aberration, caused by the scare they'd both had, fueled by the energy created by him unexpectedly finding out about her condition—and his pending fatherhood.

Tomorrow things would go back to normal. Since she had turned down his proposal, this might very well be the last time they would be together like this.

She intended to make the very most of it. She had a feeling that the memory of tonight was going to have to last her a very long time.

The next moment, he was kissing her again and her mind stopped functioning altogether.

Chapter 15

The first rays of the morning sun slipped slowly in through the slight part between the two curtains, painting sections of the bedroom in soft golden hues.

Most of the time, mornings represented a new beginning and a sense of hope for Elizabeth.

This morning, however, was different.

This morning she woke up to find herself more confused than she'd ever been in her life. On the one hand, she had her principles, rules that she had faithfully lived by all her life.

Principles that kept her strong and on track even when her world turned chaotic.

On the other hand, she had all those conflicting feelings about Whit. She was in love with him and had been for the past five years. That side was pushing for marriage under any excuse, under any circumstances. This, while her principles insisted she stay true to her beliefs.

And smack in the middle was her baby. Above all else, she needed to do right by the baby.

A baby deserved a mother *and* a father.

But at what cost?

Should she just sell out, say yes to the man who lit up her world and never, *ever* be secure in the knowledge that he actually loved her? Or ever would love her? Even if he said the words, would she be able to believe him? She just didn't know.

Elizabeth's head began to hurt.

She needed to think, to really *think* this over carefully.

Elizabeth knew she couldn't do that lying beside him this way. Just being in the same room with Whit caused her mind to come to a grinding halt, never mind the fact that they were in bed together, as nude as the days they were born.

No, if she was going to think this through and hopefully come up with an answer that she was willing and able to live with, she needed to think about it away from Whit.

Away from *all* distractions.

And then it came to her. She knew where to go

to be alone with her thoughts, to clear her mind and look at everything from a clean perspective.

Watching Whit's face closely for any indication that he was waking up, Elizabeth eased out of bed almost in slow motion. Still watching him, she gathered up the clothes she had left discarded on her chair. Holding her breath, she silently hurried into them. Then, moving on tiptoe, her boots clutched against her chest, she slipped out of the bedroom.

Making her way down the stairs, she set her sights on the front door.

She was almost home free when she ran into Carson.

He looked just as surprised to see her as she was to see him. "You're up early," he commented.

"I've got a lot on my mind," she told him, and that was the truth. Still, she mentally crossed her fingers that he wouldn't ask her to elaborate. "And I thought I'd go for a ride on one of the horses, if that's all right."

"Sure. Knock yourself out," Carson told her. "Do you need help saddling up?" he asked. He glanced around for a flat surface on which to rest the mug of coffee he was nursing in order to accompany her to the barn.

But Elizabeth shook her head. "No, but thank you for offering, though."

"Are you sure?" he pressed. "Those saddles aren't all that light."

She smiled at his comment. "I'll be fine. I grew up on a ranch. My uncle's place," she explained. "It wasn't nearly as grand or as fine as this ranch, but we did have a couple of horses. It was my job to keep them groomed and to exercise them."

What might have been a tedious chore to someone else had been a source of soothing peace for her. In those days, she was never happier than when she was on the back of a horse, with the wind in her hair and the sun on her face.

"Guess you're all set, then," Carson told her. "Have fun." Still holding the mug of coffee, he made his way toward the den, his mind elsewhere already.

A day into her stay at Adair Acres, she had discovered the barn and the horses that were stabled there. She had been completely mesmerized by the palomino stallion, Golden Thunder. Whit had told her she was free to ride the horse whenever she wanted to—as long as he came with her.

She knew that was the bodyguard in him talking and she appreciated his concern. But right now, she didn't want Whit coming along with her, since he was the problem she was hoping to work out.

Elizabeth made her way over to Thunder now,

talking softly so that the stallion could get used to her presence before she began to saddle him.

"How are you doing, boy?" she asked, gently petting the stallion's nose. To her delight, the horse seemed to recognize her. So much so that he nudged her, his attention focused exclusively on the pockets of her jeans. "Sorry, boy. No lumps of sugar on me this time. This is a spur-of-the-moment visit—"

She grinned. "If you'll pardon the pun. I've really got to clear my head, Thunder. But to do it, I'm going to need your help. I just don't know what to do," she confessed. Leaning her head against the stallion, she patted his muzzle. "Part of me wants to stay here, to marry Whit and become part of a family. But another part of me feels like I'm selling out. Following my heart instead of my head." She sighed, straightening up. "Ever have days like that?"

She looked around for the horse's saddle. She knew she could always ride Thunder bareback. She'd done it more often than not on her uncle's ranch. But if for some reason the stallion got spooked, there was more of a danger of her sliding off his back if she didn't have a saddle. She knew she had to be careful.

She was very fortunate that her fall down the stairs hadn't hurt her baby, but she knew that she shouldn't try to push her luck. Luck had a fickle habit of running out just at the wrong time.

"Where do they keep your reins and saddle, boy?" she asked Thunder as she continued looking around.

Just then, though she had her back to it, she thought she heard the barn door being closed. She'd deliberately left it open to let in the natural light. The door had closed too securely to have been accidentally shut by the wind.

With daylight being shut out, the interior of the barn would have been thrown into darkness—except for the sudden burst of light that erupted right in front of the barn door.

"Hello? Is anyone here?" Elizabeth called out. She hurried toward the entrance, but stopped abruptly when she saw the flames.

Someone had thrown a lit torch into the barn just before shutting the door. A sense of panic threatened to seize her.

Stay calm, stay calm. You're dead if you fall to pieces. And so are the horses.

Circumventing the growing flames, she managed to reach a section of the barn door. When she tried to push it open, she found that it wouldn't give. Using both hands gave her the same results.

Someone had locked the barn door from the outside.

Panic worked its way through her. She knew she

couldn't give in to it. If she did, she was a dead woman. She had to focus on escaping before the smoke got to be too much for her.

Elizabeth looked around for anything to help her.

Grabbing a shovel that had been used to muck out the stalls, she held on to the shaft as if it was a bat and swung at the barn door with all her might. Over and over she continued hitting the door in the same place, hoping that she could weaken the wood enough to make it break just enough for her to be able to get her hands on it and bend it back. All she needed was an opening.

Coughing, her eyes smarting, she kept swinging. The horses were panicking and their whinnying sounded dangerously like screams to her.

She kept swinging, her arms feeling like lead weights. When she heard the *crack* she could have cried.

When he reached for her, his eyes still closed against the morning light, Whit's hand came in contact with nothing except the comforter.

Opening his eyes, he saw that her side of the bed was empty.

The clock on the nightstand told him it was still fairly early.

"Elizabeth?" he called out.

No one answered.

Picking his head up, he looked toward the bathroom and saw that the door was wide-open.

So much for Elizabeth not hearing him because she was in the shower, he thought.

So where was she?

Whit sat up, the sheet pooling around him. He dragged his hand through his hair, trying to focus his still half-asleep brain.

The first thing that came to him was last night.

Vivid details suddenly came rushing back to him and he smiled to himself as he relived every moment, every nuance.

The discovery he'd made by the end of the night had overwhelmed him—and scared the hell out of him. But in a good way.

Each time he'd made love to her, it seemed better than the last time. *Was* better than the last time. He wasn't accustomed to that, to being surprised over and over again by the same woman. Moreover, he really wasn't accustomed to *wanting* the same woman over and over again, he mused.

The same—but different.

He rather liked that.

Whit slid his hand along her side of the bed. The area was still warm.

She hadn't been gone that long, he judged. Maybe she'd gone downstairs for breakfast. He needed to find her, to repeat his proposal and convince Elizabeth to marry him.

Determined to succeed even though he still didn't really know how he was going to convince her, Whit got dressed quickly.

He'd just pulled on his boots when he heard an alarm being sounded. Even without knowing why the alarm was going off, he suddenly felt his gut twisting almost into a knot.

Elizabeth!

He needed to find Elizabeth!

He flew out of the bedroom and down the stairs. The front door was standing wide-open and he saw members of the household staff running outside.

He grabbed the person closest to him. It turned out to be the cook. "What's going on?" he wanted to know.

"The barn is on fire!"

He wasn't sure if it was the cook who had answered him or if it was one the staff members who were running out the door, intent on fighting the fire. It didn't matter. There was only one thing that mattered—the fire had to be put out before it spread across the grounds and reached the main house.

The wind was already picking up. Whit prayed that wasn't an ominous sign.

Breaking into a run, he made it from the main house to the barn in what felt like both nothing flat and a century.

Whit could see the smoke and the flames long before he reached it.

The barn door looked like it had been broken open, the wood splintered and cracked in the middle. The horses that were kept stabled there were streaming out of the barn. The terrified sounds they made mingled with the crackle of the fire, forming an eerie, frightening cacophony.

When he saw his brother, Whit immediately hurried over to him. In all the years that they had lived here, there'd never been a fire, even during the driest of times.

"How did this start?" he wanted to know.

But Carson had no answers. "Beats me." He was busy manning one of the giant fire extinguishers that were kept on the ranch just for this sort of an emergency. It was the first time one had been put to use.

The fire department had been called, but everyone knew that the few minutes between the call and the firemen's arrival could well be crucial. They had industrial-size extinguishers, and a fire hydrant had been installed on the property just for such an eventuality. Their late father had left nothing to chance if he could help it.

The irony of this being put to use after his untimely death was not lost on Whit. The man might be gone, but his foresight lived on.

"Did you get all the horses out?" Whit asked

one of the ranch hands. The flow of horses had abruptly terminated. There was a goodly number in the corral now, but it was impossible for him to get a head count at the present time.

"I think there's a complete count," the ranch hand replied, then added, "I was just going to double-check, sir."

Whit nodded his thanks. "Do that, Diego. Meanwhile, I'm going to—"

He didn't get to finish his sentence. It was almost impossible to talk with his jaw practically on the ground. It had dropped the moment he saw the bedraggled figure emerging from the barn.

Elizabeth!

Even at this distance he could see that the smoke had left its mark all over her face and clothing. In addition, she was coughing fitfully as she stumbled out of the burning building.

Forgetting everything else, his heart pounding wildly, Whit ran over to her. He made it just in time to catch her. Her legs had buckled beneath her without any warning.

He knew she was still in danger, he just *knew* it. Very gently, he carried her away from the highly trafficked area in front of the barn. Picking a place where they wouldn't be in the way, or assaulted with questions, he lowered her to the ground and sank down beside her.

Having her life threatened twice in two days

was almost more than he could handle. "Elizabeth, what were you doing in there?" he cried.

He was struggling between wanting to hug her to him in overwhelming relief and wanting to shake her because she'd almost gotten herself killed—again.

"Trying to stay alive," she told him in between coughing fitfully.

He saw his sister and beckoned her over. "Get me some water for Elizabeth."

Landry's eyes were huge as she stared at the other woman. "What happened to her?"

"That's what I'm hoping she'll tell me after she gets her water," he told Landry.

His sister dashed off to get the water.

The moment she left, Whit turned his attention back to the woman he realized he had almost lost to the fire.

"What happened?" he wanted to know. "Did you accidentally knock over something in there?" Even as he asked the question, he realized that unless she had brought something flammable— like an old kerosene lantern—with her, there was nothing in the barn to knock over that could have caused this blaze.

The sound of sirens grew louder as Elizabeth answered in a raspy voice, "Someone threw in a torch and locked the doors."

She said the words so softly, Whit honestly

couldn't hear her the first time. He bent his head so that his ear was next to her mouth. "Could you repeat that?" he requested.

Elizabeth took a deep breath, desperately trying to get the harsh, oppressive feeling of smoke out of her lungs. After a moment, she repeated what she'd said. "Someone threw in a torch—just before they locked the barn door."

Whit looked at her, dumbfounded. He had trouble processing what she'd just said. She was talking about arson, as well as attempted murder and just possibly the attempted slaughter of the ranch's herd of horses. Here, at Adair Acres. That meant that someone on the inside was responsible.

"Are you sure?" he pressed, shaken.

"I'm sure," she replied stoically. "I saw the flames starting. And when I pushed the door, it wouldn't open. Someone had locked it from the outside. I found a shovel and started beating against the door with it until the wood finally cracked." Shaking her head, she just couldn't understand. Elizabeth looked at him, her brow furrowed. "Why would someone want to kill those horses?"

"It wasn't the horses that they were trying to kill," he replied, his eyes on hers. "The horses would have just been collateral damage."

Just then, Landry returned with a glass of water for Elizabeth. Offering the glass to the other woman, her hand shook slightly when she heard the last of Elizabeth's statement and what her brother said in reply. Landry exchanged looks with Whit.

"Mother," she said, stunned and numbed at the same time.

"Mother what?" he wanted to know. His eyes never left Landry's face.

This wasn't easy for her. All her life, she had done everything her mother asked of her. She'd gone to the schools her mother wanted her to, dated the boys her mother selected and was even now engaged to someone of her mother's choosing— someone who wasn't of her own choosing. Landry had always tried to please her mother. And now she was in a situation where she had come in conflict with the course of her whole young life.

But she had grown very fond of Elizabeth and she looked up to Whit. So she answered honestly, "I saw Mother hurrying into the house just before someone yelled that the barn was on fire."

Stunned, not wanting to believe what he was hearing—yet knowing in his heart that it had to be true—Whit took hold of his sister's shoulders and asked her, "Are you sure, Landry?"

Landry nodded. "I'm sure. She didn't see me, but I saw her. It was Mother. She ran into the house and then headed off in the direction of her private apartment."

Furious, Whit rose to his feet. Elizabeth scrambled to hers and caught his hand before he could walk away. He looked angrier than she had ever seen him look. "Where are you going?"

"If she started that fire, then our mother or not, she's going to be made to pay to the full extent of the law," he declared fiercely.

"Whit, she's your mother," Elizabeth said. "You can't do that."

"Yes, I can," he answered stoically. "Don't you realize that you could have been killed?" he asked Elizabeth.

Having said the words out loud, he was convinced that had been his mother's intention—to kill Elizabeth. What he didn't know and couldn't understand was why. Why was his mother trying to kill the woman he was involved with? Patsy had never taken an interest in any of their lives before, why the sudden change now?

What did she stand to gain by getting rid of Elizabeth? Because that was what it all had to boil down to—the way it affected Patsy. It was *always* about his mother, no matter what.

"I know, but I wasn't killed," Elizabeth pointed out patiently. "And the horses are safe. Maybe if you just talk to her, you can work things out to your satisfaction," she suggested.

"Oh, I'll talk to my mother all right," he told her. He began to stride toward the house, only to realize that Elizabeth was hurrying right behind him, trying to catch up.

He stopped and swung around to face her. "Where are you going?" he demanded.

"With you," she answered with no hesitation.

"No, you're not," he said with finality. Things could get very ugly and he didn't want her to have to witness that. She'd already been through more than enough in his opinion.

"Yes, I am," Elizabeth insisted. She was not about to back down. "Someone's got to be there to stop you from doing something stupid. I'm not going to have my baby have to visit his or her father in prison."

He stared at her in disbelief. Just how forgiving was this woman? "My mother just tried to kill you. Not the horses—*you*," he all but shouted.

In her heart, she knew that. She just hadn't wanted to face it immediately. "So I have more of a say what happens to her than you do," she said.

Whit shook his head, surrendering this round to her. "You are a damn stubborn woman."

"Yes, I am," she agreed, then added with the smallest of smiles, "Deal with it."

Whit looked at her for a long moment. "I will— I want to. I want to for the rest of my life." These past few minutes had made him see his life in a whole new light. Made him realize things about himself that he hadn't even been aware of. "If anything had happened to you in that barn—I don't know what I would have done."

"You would have dealt with it," she told him simply. "And gotten over it."

"No, I wouldn't have." He took her hands in his as he swore, "Ever."

With that, he dropped her hands, turned on his heel and continued back to the house.

It was all Elizabeth could do to keep up with him. But she did. Now was *not* the time to fall behind. All sorts of questions were popping up in her mind, but despite the dire situation and what she had just endured, she couldn't help smiling.

In the end, everything would be all right.

She could just *feel* it.

Chapter 16

"Mother!" Whit called out as he entered the suite of rooms that Patsy Adair had taken to occupying more than a decade ago. "Mother, get down here! Now! Trust me, you are not going to be happy if I have to go upstairs to get you," he promised angrily.

"Whit," Elizabeth chided, trying to get him to rein in his temper.

"She can't be allowed to get away with this, Elizabeth," he told her firmly. Elizabeth had much too kind a heart, he thought. But his mother had really crossed the line this time, and he wasn't about to look the other way any longer. "Now, Mother!"

The next moment, Patsy appeared at the landing. She assumed the stance of a queen regally looking down at her subjects.

She was far from pleased at the tone he was using, especially in front of a woman she thought was her late husband's mistress.

"I am your mother, Whit, and you will show me respect," she informed him coldly.

"Respect?" Whit echoed in disbelief. "You mean the way *you* show respect for everyone else?"

"Change your tone this instant, Whit. I don't answer to you," Patsy told him haughtily.

Whit took a couple of steps up the stairs, cold fury in his eyes. The fire department had arrived and the fire was being dealt with, but it could have been so much worse.

"Well, you're sure as hell going to have to answer to someone for what you've done."

Patsy's eyes narrowed as she glared at Elizabeth, then shifted that look back to her son. "She has you believing her lies now, does she? The king is dead, long live the king—is that your little game, whore?" Patsy demanded, all but shouting the words into Elizabeth's face.

Patsy reached the bottom step, crowding her son out of the way. "Your father was carrying on with her for years. I finally had enough of it and hired a private detective to follow this two-bit tart around. She and your father spent a hell of a lot of time 'working together' after hours. Given your father's appetites, it's not hard to put two and two together even if the PI couldn't manage to get any compromising pictures of them. He did hack into her medical file, though. Did you know that she's pregnant with your father's bastard?"

"Watch your mouth, Mother. And that's *not* Dad's baby," Whit informed her coldly.

"Of course it is!" Patsy shouted angrily. "That was what your father did—he went around impregnating floozies. Spreading his seed. That's how that worthless Ruby got her hooks into him. Too bad for her the kid disappeared after three months. But if he hadn't, you might never have been born," she informed Whit arrogantly.

"Do you have *any* idea how hard I had to fight to make sure that no one else got their hands on our money? I had Ruby's funds frozen, and as for this latest little twist," she sneered, slanting a glance at Elizabeth's abdomen, "a lot of things can happen before this conniving schemer's due date."

Whit had no idea where to begin in order to set his mother straight. He sincerely doubted he could. And at this point, it didn't really matter. He just wanted her dealt with and put away. "You're a sick woman," he informed Patsy. "You're absolutely insane. A paranoid woman making up fantastical stories."

Patsy tossed her head, her overly blond hair swishing back and forth from the momentum.

"Correction, Whit. I'm a smart woman who intends to get everything that's coming to her."

"Count on it, Mother," Whit told her. With that, he turned his back on her. Taking Elizabeth's hand in his, he said, "Let's go, Elizabeth. I don't want you breathing in any more of this toxic air. It's bad for the baby."

"Go ahead, walk away," Patsy shouted after her son. "But you know I'm right. I only did what had to be done. I saved this family! You'd all be ruined if it wasn't for me!"

"Do you know what she's talking about?" Elizabeth asked him.

"Not a clue," Whit told her. He deliberately locked the door from the outside, then dragged a chair that was against one of the walls in the hallway and wedged it against the doorknob. "There, that should hold her."

"Whit, what are you doing?" his mother shouted from the other side of the door. It rattled back and forth as she tried to turn the doorknob and open the door. "You unlock this door, Whit! Open it right now, do you hear me?" she demanded, screaming.

He made no answer as he walked away.

"What are you going to do?" Elizabeth wanted to know as they made their way to the other side of the house and away from Patsy's quarters.

"What I said I'd do." He spared his mother's part of the house one final glance before squaring his shoulders and moving on. "Have her arrested."

Elizabeth looked at him skeptically. "Isn't that a little harsh?"

He was right. Elizabeth *was* too kind and definitely too forgiving.

"She almost *killed* you. *That's* harsh," Whit pointed out. "I'm also beginning to think that she might have killed my father."

Completely stunned, Elizabeth stopped walking. "Really?"

"Think about it," he told her. "All that anger and resentment building up inside of her all this time. She pushed you down the stairs either to kill you or cause you to have a miscarriage. When that didn't work, she locked you in the barn and set it on fire. Shooting my father close up would have been a piece of cake for her. I wouldn't put *anything* past her," he said with feeling. "I don't think you're going to be safe until she's locked up."

"But she's your mother," Elizabeth protested again. "You can't have your own mother locked up like that." Although, she had to admit the idea of putting the woman behind bars would make her feel a whole lot safer.

He could and he would, Whit thought. And then maybe they could sleep again at night.

"She's not a mother, she's a she-wolf," he told

Elizabeth simply. Reaching the foyer, he took out his phone to make the call to the police. "And if I have to choose between her and you, there's no contest. I pick you—in a heartbeat."

Elizabeth would have loved to believe that love was what motivated him, but she was afraid to think that way. What if she were wrong? She wouldn't be able to stand the disappointment.

"Because I'm carrying your baby," she guessed, nodding her head.

He canceled the call he'd started to make. This had to be cleared up first. Elizabeth had to believe him. "No, because I love you."

Elizabeth stared at him, almost speechless. This was too good to believe. "I thought you said that you didn't think you *could* love someone."

"I didn't think I could, but, as it turns out, I was wrong. Very wrong," he told her. "Those few minutes when I realized that you were in that barn, that you might very well be…"

He couldn't bring himself to finish his sentence. "Well, I suddenly found myself praying that you were all right, that if you somehow came out of all this in one piece, then I was going to spend the rest of my life trying to make you happy."

There were tears in her eyes now. He meant it—she could tell that he meant it. It was all she could do to stifle the sob that rose in her throat.

"You already have," she said just before she kissed him.

Whit allowed himself one very long moment to savor the taste of her lips. The taste of love. And then he drew back.

"Much as I'd love to continue this line of conversation, I need to get the police out here." He winked at her just before he pressed 9-1-1. "To be continued," he promised.

Detective Otis Kramer arrived on the scene quickly. Still in charge of the initial murder investigation surrounding Reginald Adair, the detective was open to any possible new leads that might help him finally close his case.

He listened carefully to Whit's account of what had been going on, especially this latest development with his mother.

Whit had been joined by Landry and Carson, both of whom backed up what he had to say about the fire, as well as Elizabeth's orchestrated fall down the stairs. Elizabeth gave her own statement describing how she'd felt hands against her back just before she fell and that she had also caught a whiff of Patsy's expensive perfume. Landry told the detective that she had seen her mother hurrying away from the barn only a couple minutes before it burst into flames.

Kramer listened to everything, jotting things

down furiously but making no comment until everyone had had their say.

"And you're sure about this?" the detective asked once everyone had given their statements. His question was clearly aimed at Landry, because she was the only one who had seen Patsy running from the barn.

It clearly pained Landry to confirm what she had just said, but she did. It made her feel disloyal to her mother, but she knew that she couldn't allow her mother to continue to be a threat to everyone, especially to Elizabeth.

"All right," Kramer said, tucking his worn notepad into his oversized, misshapen pocket. "I have enough to take your mother in for questioning," he told the four people around him. He waved the police backup he'd brought with him toward Patsy's separate quarters.

The officer returned alone.

"Well, where's Mrs. Adair?" Kramer asked the officer sharply.

The officer, Samuel Ortiz, a tall, imposing man in his forties, had almost a foot on the detective. But right now, he looked hapless.

"She's gone, Detective."

"Gone?" Kramer repeated incredulously. "What do you mean, gone?" he demanded.

"We just left her in her suite," Elizabeth told the

detective. "Whit locked the door so she couldn't get out."

But the officer shook his head. "Well, she must've gotten out somehow. She wasn't there, sir," he repeated. "I checked everywhere. I even knocked on the powder room door," he told the man who gave him his orders.

Incensed, angry at himself for not keeping tabs on his mother when he *knew* how very dangerous she could be—how dangerous she *was*—Whit hurried past the detective and the officer to check out the rooms for himself.

He took the stairs two at a time, moving as quickly as he could. Swearing at himself under his breath.

When he arrived in the quarters where he had confronted his mother less than ten minutes ago, Whit found them to be unoccupied.

The door to her walk-in closet was standing open and it looked as if a few things had been taken. Most likely hastily tossed into a suitcase, he guessed.

In any event, his mother had apparently taken off, choosing to run rather than remain and either clear her name—or take her punishment.

Entering behind Whit and Elizabeth, Landry immediately crossed over to the massive bureau. Her mother's jewelry box was pushed over to the side and no longer closed. Landry carefully lifted up the center layer, where her mother kept all her different rings. Beneath that was a small bottom drawer. It was different than the rest in appearance.

The drawer, normally locked, wasn't this time.

Landry opened the drawer and looked inside. It was empty.

"I don't think you're going to be able to find Mother very easily," she said, turning to Whit.

"What makes you say that?" Elizabeth asked, looking into the jewelry box, as well.

For the most part, it looked as if Patsy had left everything. That struck her as odd, thinking that the woman could have definitely pawned or sold a few items if she needed ready cash quickly. Any piece there looked to be a fortune.

"Mother kept her passport in the bottom drawer of her jewelry box," Landry answered. "It's gone. That means that—"

"—she could be anywhere in the world," Whit concluded in disgust.

Kramer sighed, frustrated. "Looks like we're out of luck," he said. "My jurisdiction ends outside of San Diego County." Which meant that he had to hustle to catch Patsy before she left the area. There was little to no satisfaction in notifying the proper authorities in another state, much less in another country, if Patsy made good her escape. Apprehending her could get very messy.

The detective turned toward Landry. "You got

a picture of your mom I could use? If we send this to all the airlines with flights leaving the country, maybe we'll get lucky and have someone detain her until I get there," Kramer said.

"I've got one right here on my phone," Landry told the detective. "Here," she offered, "let me send it to you."

As the detective gave her his cell number, they all heard a commotion coming from the first floor near the front door. The sound of raised, angry voices carried upstairs, but Whit wasn't able to make out what was being said.

Whit exchanged glances with Elizabeth. "This day just keeps getting better and better," he declared sarcastically. "If you need me, Detective, I'll be downstairs, trying to get to the bottom of whatever's going on down there," he tossed over his shoulder as he made his way to the commotion.

Elizabeth was quick to follow him.

Though neither of them knew exactly how, Carson had somehow managed to get there ahead of him.

His brother was talking to two women. They looked to be mother and daughter, from what Whit could see. If he had to take a guess, the thin, almost fragile older woman looked to be around his mother's age, perhaps a little older. She certainly looked far less flamboyant than Patsy—more down-to-earth than his mother ever had been.

The younger one was the fiery one of the duo, with long dark red hair and green eyes that right now seemed to be shooting sparks aimed at his brother.

"What's going on?" Whit asked Carson even as he looked from one woman to the other.

The older woman spoke first.

"I'm Ruby Adair Mason—your late father's ex-wife," the woman introduced herself in a soft, non-confrontational voice.

No such restrictions hampered the younger woman. "And your witch of a mother won't release the money due my stepmother. We've come to claim what's rightfully hers," she concluded, nodding at the older woman.

"Hey, wait a minute," Carson said crisply. "You can't just barge in here without any warning. We didn't even get your name."

"That's because I didn't give it," the younger woman retorted between teeth that were fairly clenched. It was obvious that she did *not* want to be here.

"Georgia." Ruby laid her hand on the young woman's arm. "We didn't come here to fight."

"*You* didn't," Georgia corrected, although her voice lost its confrontational tone when she spoke to her stepmother. "I made no such promise. Your mother," she informed the trio before her, obviously mistaking Elizabeth for Landry, "has done nothing but create trouble for my stepmother whenever the opportunity came up. Now personally, I wouldn't accept a gum wrapper from you people, but if nothing else, my stepmother deserves that money your father left her to cover all the pain and suffering she'd gone through at the hands of your father's holier-than-thou family."

She looked from Carson to Whit. "So we've come to get the money in person. I'd like to wrap this up as soon as possible, please."

"Is there a problem here?" Kramer asked, joining them just before he prepared to leave the premises. Officer Ortiz was hovering nearby, waiting for instructions.

"Nothing we can't take care of on our own, Detective," Whit assured the man.

That was just fine with the detective. He already had enough to contend with. "Then I'll see if I can find your mother before she flees the country."

His tone didn't hold much promise, Elizabeth thought.

"Wait, your mother's fleeing the country?" Georgia cried, looking from one brother to the other. It was clear that this news did not sit well with her.

"Long story," Whit told her, dismissing it for now.

Georgia frowned. "This is a family of long stories," she commented. The comment definitely wasn't meant as a compliment.

As the detective and his backup let themselves out, both brothers turned their attention to the older of the two women.

Whit scrutinized Ruby Mason for a long moment. "Are you Jackson's mother?" he finally asked.

The pain was immediate, etching itself into her face as if it had been there just beneath the surface all along and would always remain there as well.

Ruby raised her head proudly, recalling the child fate had not allowed her to raise.

"I am. I was," she corrected herself as she sighed deeply.

"My father mentioned Jackson in his will," Whit told her. "He's to get a quarter of the family business."

Ruby nodded her head. "Yes, I know. Your father's lawyer sent me a copy of that section, as well as the section referring to the money Reginald left to me."

She had been surprised, to say the least, to discover that she was in her ex-husband's will. It told her that he *had* cared for her after all, at least a little. The fact that he had left a portion of his empire to their son was far less of a surprise. Reginald had always held fast to the belief that the boy was still out there somewhere, alive and completely in the dark as to who he really was.

"If you don't mind, ma'am, we'd like to ask you

some questions about Jackson," Carson told her, barely controlling his eagerness. "We've been trying to find him, too."

It was obvious that he believed that pooling their information could very well help them locate their missing older brother.

"I think she needs to rest a little first," Elizabeth said, speaking up for the first time since Ruby and her stepdaughter had arrived. "They both do," she said to Whit. "Heaven knows there are enough guest rooms here. Why don't you put them up in one, let them freshen up and then when they've rested, they can answer your questions," she suggested.

Whit laughed, tucking one arm around her and drawing Elizabeth closer to him. Even as he did so, he silently reveled in the overwhelming happiness he felt pervading all through him.

Georgia put up a hand. "No need. I only came by to tell you that I plan to arrange a mediation meeting with an attorney who specializes in will disputes. I'm sure you can see why this would be necessary."

"Of course," Carson indulged the woman.

Ruby looked around uncomfortably, no doubt embarrassed by her stepdaughter's blunt behavior. But before she could do anything, Georgia looped her arm through Ruby's and showed their way out.

"I tried," Elizabeth said helplessly, looking around at the group.

"You spoke like a true lady of the manor already," Whit teased, whispering the words into Elizabeth's ear. "I'm proud of you."

She blushed slightly, even though she knew that the others hadn't heard what Whit said.

She also didn't say anything to deny the assumption that Whit had made by voicing his simple comment. That she was going to accept the proposal he had first tendered to her yesterday. Accept it gladly—but only because of what he had said to her *after* she had escaped the fire.

That he realized that he loved her.

That was all she'd ever wanted, to be loved by someone whom *she* loved.

Sometimes a person had to face hell first in order to gain heaven, Elizabeth thought. She couldn't speak for others, but in her case, she felt it was well worth it.

Well worth it.

Epilogue

Despite Whit's chiding and his reminders that there were people on the staff who could and *would* take care of all these details for her, Elizabeth insisted that she wanted to be hands-on when it came to throwing what was going to be their very first party.

As per her request, Whit had invited a small number of family and friends to the party, telling them that this was a spur-of-the-moment, impromptu gathering with nothing fancy planned.

Elizabeth was wearing herself out getting ready for "nothing fancy."

"You know, the cook is called that for a reason, Elizabeth," he pointed out as he attempted to follow her around the kitchen without getting trampled when she made sudden changes of direction.

When she turned around and was about to sail past him to get to the pantry, he caught her in his arms and held on. He kissed her forehead affectionately.

"By the time everyone arrives, you're going to be too exhausted to enjoy the party—and the reason for it," he told her.

"I want it to be perfect," she insisted, easing herself out of his hold. This time she made it to the pantry.

"And it will be," he assured her, following her once again. "Because you'll be there."

That stopped her.

Turning around, she looked at him. "I think that is the sweetest thing I've ever heard you say."

"Stick around, I'm just getting warmed up," he promised with a warm, sexy wink.

"Oh, I intend to stick around, Mr. Adair," she replied. "For a very, very long time."

"I will hold you to that," he told her. "Until then, I'll just hold you," he said, taking her into his arms for a second time.

Again she managed to wiggle out of his embrace. "After the party," she told him, hurrying over to the counter. She began taking things out of the refrigerator. She needed to get started on the appetizers. "You can hold me all you want *after* the party. But until then, there's still so much to do." A thought suddenly hit her. "You did remember to tell Ruby and her stepdaughter that they're invited, too, didn't you?"

"I did," he told her solemnly. "Georgia declined," he said with a slight shake of his head. "I tried to talk her out of it, but she insisted. I'm sure for Ruby, all the bad blood between her and my family is in the past, but as for Georgia, I think she wants to do battle with and string up every Adair she encounters to avenge the way Dad's family treated Ruby when they were married."

Word had it that his grandparents had been rude and belittling to Ruby because she didn't have the proper bloodlines. He could well believe it.

Elizabeth paused for a moment, shaking her head. "That must have been really rough on poor Ruby." She looked up into Whit's eyes. "I sympathize with her completely."

"I know what you're thinking, but it's not like that with my family." He kissed the side of her temple, doing his best to hold himself in check— for now. "Good thing you're so likable."

"Your mother hates me," she reminded him.

His face clouded over for a moment. "I have no mother," he informed her.

The police hadn't caught Patsy, who, rumor had it, had taken off for Europe. He sincerely hoped that the woman had sense enough to stay far, far away from the house and any of them—especially Elizabeth.

And then he brightened, changing the subject. "Since I can't get you to relax, I might as well help you. What do you want me to do?"

Elizabeth paused as she grinned at him. "I thought you'd never ask."

It had taken a lot of work.

In the end, she had utilized most of the household staff, reluctantly giving in to Whit's entreaties, strictly because she didn't want to overdo things in case that affected the baby. But the house was finally decorated for the party, the appetizers were all out and warm, and the bar was open and being manned by one of the ranch hands, who really knew his way around mixed drinks and straight alcohol. In addition, the cake had been made and was in the refrigerator, and the main course had been prepared.

All that remained was for the party to begin.

"It all looks great, doesn't it?" she asked Whit, gesturing around the newly decorated living room.

Just then, the doorbell rang.

Their first guests were arriving.

"It looks nice," Whit corrected her. "*You* look great."

"You are definitely a better fiancé than you were a boss," she told him, her eyes sparkling.

"Just wait, the evening's still very young. I get better," he whispered, then gave her another sexy wink as they went to answer the door together.

Guests kept trickling in, a few early, some on time and others fashionably late. But eventually, everyone who'd been on their guest list had arrived.

Whit had just picked up a glass of champagne and called for everyone's attention. But before he could say another word, the doorbell rang again. Since he and Elizabeth had invited everyone they wanted to be here and those people were now gathered in the living room, Whit had no idea who else might have picked this time to come to pay them a social call.

"Everyone hold on to your champagne," Whit instructed. "This won't take long." With that, he made his way to the front door.

Curious as to who was there, Elizabeth was right beside him.

Whit opened the door, about to dismiss whoever was on the other side of the door and send them away.

"Heard you were throwing a party. Thought I'd crash it," the tall, dark blond–haired young man with the bright blue eyes said.

Whit was quick to recover. He hugged the well-built man with one arm, holding his champagne aloft with his free hand.

"Wow, you are a sight for sore eyes. Nobody expected you for at least another couple of weeks—if not longer," he said. Then, suddenly remembering his manners, he turned toward Elizabeth. "Elizabeth, this jack-of-all-trades nomad is my cousin Noah. My aunt Emmaline's son," he added. "Dad left part ownership of the ranch to him," he reminded her.

"I remember. Nice to meet you, Noah," she said, shaking the other man's hand.

She couldn't get over how much Whit and his cousin looked alike. Oh, their hair was different, but their eyes were the same color and their profiles were strikingly similar. But then, she knew that Noah's mother was Whit's father's sister, so a family resemblance was to be expected, she thought.

She smiled at Noah warmly. "Welcome to the party."

"Grab a glass of champagne," Whit urged his cousin. "I was just about to make a toast—and an announcement."

"You've twisted my arm," Noah answered wryly, corralling the nearest server and plucking a glass of champagne from the man's tray.

Taking Elizabeth's hand, Whit worked his way back to the center of the crowd.

"I'm glad you could all make it," he began. "Elizabeth and I have a little announcement to make. Actually, two," he amended. "The first announcement is that, thanks to this lovely lady beside me, I'm going to be a dad."

Congratulations began flying left and right as the people converged around them hugging, kissing and voicing their well-wishing.

Whit gave it a couple minutes before he called for everyone to quiet down. "I'm not finished yet," he went on.

"You're expecting twins?" someone in the group cracked.

"Not that I know of," Whit answered. "No, since you all are the closest thing we have to friends—"

His wisecrack was greeted with other wisecracks. Laughing, he held up his hand. "Okay, okay, I confess, you're all very important to us. So important that we wanted to share something else with you."

"Diaper duty?" another voice yelled out.

"No, our wedding. Which is why we decided to get married here, tonight, in front of all of you," Whit told them.

Voices rose again as more congratulations came from everyone there, mingling with other words that were filled with good wishes and kindly jabs.

This time, Whit made no effort to quiet the crowd. Instead he and Elizabeth stood in the center of their family and friends and absorbed every last sound, every last hug.

Both of them could feel the love permeating from the crowd—and from each other.

No man, Whit thought as he tightened his arm around Elizabeth, could have asked for more. He considered himself to be one very lucky son of a gun.

* * * * *

Don't miss Marie's next romance,
MENDOZA'S SECRET FORTUNE,
available March 2015 from
Harlequin Special Edition.

And if you loved CARRYING HIS SECRET,
you'll enjoy these other suspenseful stories from
Marie Ferrarella:

CAVANAUGH STRONG
CAVANAUGH UNDERCOVER
CAVANAUGH HERO
MISSION: CAVANAUGH BABY

Available now from
Harlequin Romantic Suspense!

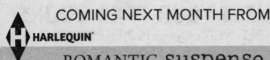

REQUEST YOUR FREE BOOKS!

2 FREE NOVELS PLUS 2 FREE GIFTS!

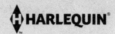

ROMANTIC suspense

Sparked by danger, fueled by passion

YES! Please send me 2 FREE Harlequin® Romantic Suspense novels and my 2 FREE gifts (gifts are worth about $10). After receiving them, if I don't wish to receive any more books, I can return the shipping statement marked "cancel." If I don't cancel, I will receive 4 brand-new novels every month and be billed just $4.74 per book in the U.S. or $5.24 per book in Canada. That's a savings of at least 14% off the cover price! It's quite a bargain! Shipping and handling is just 50¢ per book in the U.S. and 75¢ per book in Canada.* I understand that accepting the 2 free books and gifts places me under no obligation to buy anything. I can always return a shipment and cancel at any time. Even if I never buy another book, the two free books and gifts are mine to keep forever.

240/340 HDN F45N

Name _____ (PLEASE PRINT)

Address _____ Apt. #

City _____ State/Prov. _____ Zip/Postal Code

Signature (if under 18, a parent or guardian must sign)

Mail to the **Harlequin® Reader Service:**

IN U.S.A.: P.O. Box 1867, Buffalo, NY 14240-1867
IN CANADA: P.O. Box 609, Fort Erie, Ontario L2A 5X3

Want to try two free books from another line?
Call 1-800-873-8635 or visit www.ReaderService.com.

* Terms and prices subject to change without notice. Prices do not include applicable taxes. Sales tax applicable in N.Y. Canadian residents will be charged applicable taxes. Offer not valid in Quebec. This offer is limited to one order per household. Not valid for current subscribers to Harlequin Romantic Suspense books. All orders subject to credit approval. Credit or debit balances in a customer's account(s) may be offset by any other outstanding balance owed by or to the customer. Please allow 4 to 6 weeks for delivery. Offer available while quantities last.

Your Privacy—The Harlequin® Reader Service is committed to protecting your privacy. Our Privacy Policy is available online at www.ReaderService.com or upon request from the Harlequin Reader Service.

We make a portion of our mailing list available to reputable third parties that offer products we believe may interest you. If you prefer that we not exchange your name with third parties, or if you wish to clarify or modify your communication preferences, please visit us at www.ReaderService.com/consumerchoice or write to us at Harlequin Reader Service Preference Service, P.O. Box 9062, Buffalo, NY 14269. Include your complete name and address.

HRS13R

He stepped outside and looked around. "What are you doing out here all by yourself in the dark?"

"You told my son that cowboys only bathe once a week, and now Sammy won't get into the bathtub."

By the light of the room spilling out where they stood, she saw his amusement curve his lips upward. "Is that a fact?" he replied. "Sounds like a personal problem to me."

"It's all your fault," she said, at the same time trying not to notice the wonder of his broad shoulders, the slim hips that wore his jeans so well.

He raised a dark eyebrow. "The way I see it, you started it."

This time the heat that filled her cheeks was a new wave of pure embarrassment. "Look, I'm sorry. When I told my son those things, I'd never really met a cowboy before. The only cowboy I've ever even seen in my entire life is the naked singing cowboy in Times Square. I now have a little boy who refuses to take a bath. Can you please come back to the house with me and tell him differently?"

Amusement once again danced in his eyes as he gave her a smile that made her feel just a little bit breathless. "Basically you've come to say you're sorry about your preconceived notions about cowboys, because I think it would be nice if you apologized before asking for my help about anything."

"You're right. I am sorry," she replied, wondering if he wanted her to get down on her knees before him and grovel, as well.

"Okay, then, let's go." He pulled the door of his unit closed behind him and fell into step next to her.

"A naked singing cowboy…and you New Yorkers think we're strange." He laughed, a low, deep rumble that she found far too pleasant.

She realized at that moment that she wasn't afraid of cows or horses, that she wasn't worried about falling into the mud or getting her hands dirty.

The real danger came from the attraction she felt for the man who walked next to her, a man whose laughter warmed her and who smelled like spring wind and leather.

Don't miss A REAL COWBOY by Carla Cassidy,
available March 2015
wherever Harlequin® Romantic Suspense
books and ebooks are sold.

www.Harlequin.com

JUST CAN'T GET ENOUGH?

Join our social communities
and talk to us online.

You will have access to the latest
news on upcoming titles and special
promotions, but most importantly,
you can talk to other fans about your
favorite Harlequin reads.

Harlequin.com/Community

Facebook.com/HarlequinBooks

Twitter.com/HarlequinBooks

Pinterest.com/HarlequinBooks

HARLEQUIN®

A *Romance* FOR EVERY MOOD™

**Stay up-to-date on all your
romance-reading news with the
Harlequin Shopping Guide,
featuring bestselling authors, exciting new
miniseries, books to watch and more!**

The newest issue will be delivered right to you
with our compliments! There are 4 each year.

Signing up is easy.

EMAIL

ShoppingGuide@Harlequin.ca

WRITE TO US

HARLEQUIN BOOKS
Attention: Customer Service Department
P.O. Box 9057, Buffalo, NY 14269-9057

OR PHONE

1-800-873-8635 in the United States
1-888-343-9777 in Canada

Please allow 4-6 weeks for delivery of the first issue by mail.